"I slept with my best friend's boyfriend"

Our bodies entwined as we fell and my breath was completely knocked out of me. It wasn't caused by the fall, but by the sheer thrill of coming into contact with Josh's chest, arms, thighs. . . He had a firm hold of me round the waist, and he wasn't letting go. We lay there for what seemed like for ever, me with my head on his chest, feeling his hot breath on my face. He began stroking my back with his fingers, slowly and methodically. It was so erotic, it was almost unbearable. I could stay like this for ever, I thought, but I was terrified Beth would be watching. I pulled away and leapt up. It was a good job I did, because the next moment I heard Beth's voice loud and clear and very near.

Other books also available in this series:

My Sister – The Superbitch
Rosie Corrigan

They Think I'm Too Easy
Lorna Read

My Boyfriend's Older Than My Dad
Jill Eckersley

Look out for:

I Taught Him a Lesson He'll Never Forget
Amber Vane

"I slept with my best friend's boyfriend"

Sue Dando

■SCHOLASTIC

Scholastic Children's Books
Commonwealth House, 1–19 New Oxford Street,
London WC1A 1NU, UK
A division of Scholastic Ltd
London ~ New York ~ Toronto ~ Sydney ~ Auckland

First published in the UK by Scholastic Ltd, 1998

ISBN 0 590 11150 7

Typeset by Falcon Oast Graphic Art
Printed by Cox and Wyman Ltd, Reading, Berks.

10 9 8 7 6 5 4 3 2 1

Prologue

Looking back, I don't know how I managed to make such a mess of things. I mean, it's not as though Beth and I were just mates, or the sort of people who hang out together at weekends, just for someone to go around with. If we were, maybe I wouldn't feel so guilty. No, our friendship goes much deeper than that.

We've known each other since we were at primary school together, and over the years we've become, you know, inseparable, as close as best friends could possibly be. We shared our experiences on the full range of stuff life throws at you, from periods to spots to first snogs to dates to – well, everything really.

It got to the stage where we sometimes didn't even have to talk to communicate, which made us so irritating to anyone not included in our little clique, namely the rest of the world. When we did talk more often than not we finished each other's sentences; we'd collapse into fits of silly giggles at the same stupid things; we'd spend all day together at school, then talk on the phone for hours at night. We had the same taste in clothes and music, and we drooled over the same boy bands.

Physically, we're very different. Beth is a total babe, so stunning she wouldn't look out of place on the *Baywatch* beach – the only difference being that she has a brain. She's got long blonde hair, cornflower blue eyes and an absolutely lovely personality. Because of her looks I learned many years ago that guys usually asked her out in preference to me. As far as I was concerned that was cool, because there was an unwritten rule between us that if one of us had got the hots for a guy, the other steered well clear. Which was fine. Until Josh came along.

From the first time I set eyes on him I fancied Josh like mad. He was everything I looked for in a guy: amusing, intelligent, good fun, and absolutely drop-dead gorgeous. (It helps.) We're talking seriously divine looking here – the sort of guy who makes Brad Pitt look like a walrus. You get my drift?

When Josh hit on me at a party, I was shocked, confused, and excited all at the same time. At first I rejected his advances. But then he told me how he really felt about me, and that's when my life started to go horribly wrong.

Because the thing was, he already had a girlfriend. Beth.

Big problem.

Chapter 1

Six months earlier . . .

"Come on, Beth, hurry up. We'll be late."

I lay sprawled on the bed watching my friend as she rummaged frantically through her wardrobe, her front end disappearing ever further inside as she burrowed deep into a pile of clothes. As each item was discarded, it was unceremoniously hurled into the room, accompanied by a muffled "Damn!", or an "Oh, bum!", followed by more digging.

"I know it's in here somewhere," she grunted, huffing as she added, "I remember putting it away just last week."

"Do you *have* to wear the blue top? Can't you wear the yellow? The yellow looks great on you." I was pleading now, knowing that Beth's "putting it away" actually meant "lobbing it in no particular direction and then forgetting about it for weeks on end", and that the chances of her finding the top this side of Christmas were pretty remote. But no; on this particular evening, for this particular occasion, of all the hundreds of outfits she possessed, only the blue top would do. And if she didn't hurry up, we really *were* going to be late.

However infuriating Beth was being, I couldn't blame her for wanting to look perfect tonight. We were going to the opening night of the first branch of the Style Café to be opened outside London. Some of the Supermodels were patrons of the place and rumoured to be putting in an appearance, and it was what everyone under the age of thirty considered to be our town's last chance to shed its dull-as-ditchwater image and become a happening place. Invites were at a premium, and while all our mates were going along, they'd be left hanging around outside, pressing their ticketless noses to the windows.

Beth and I, on the other hand, along with loads of invited celebrities (she said hopefully), would waltz past security on the door and glide inside. I couldn't wait. It didn't matter that we'd only got tickets by default. Beth's sister, Angie, was a fashion designer in London and had passed her invites down to "little sis" as a "treat". Since moving to Notting Hill, Angie considered anything happening outside the capital to be too naff to even contemplate, and the fact that she'd been invited to a party in her home town repulsed her even more. Which was great for us, because it meant we got to go instead.

"Ha! Got it!" Beth's voice was triumphant as she clambered backwards out of the wardrobe, holding up a piece of aquamarine Lycra no bigger than a duster.

"Thank God for that!" I muttered as she whipped off her T-shirt and pulled the top on. She looked great. OK, so Beth would look fabulous in a dishcloth – she was that sort of person – but tonight, decked out in black knee-high leather boots with ten-centimetre-high heels, micro-mini, low-slung fake designer belt and her skin-tight, boob-crunching top, she looked like she'd walked off the pages of a fashion magazine. I sometimes felt like Quasimodo lumbering alongside her and I now realized that tonight would be no exception. I know I'm being hard on myself, because believe me I'm not hideous, but imagine how you'd feel if your best friend made Kate Moss look like one of the Ugly Sisters! I'm not joking.

I glanced at myself in the full-length mirror,

desperately hoping that perhaps I'd suddenly been transformed into a sexy, pouting babe who looked like an extra on the *Home and Away* beach. "More like Bognor beach," I complained as I studied the figure clad in a skimpy scarlet dress staring back at me.

I've got the kind of looks that would probably be described as "striking" or "unusual", rather than "beautiful" or "pretty". I'm certainly not blessed with the regular features and symmetrical face that models and girls on the telly always seem to have. I think of myself as more of an acquired taste: guys don't automatically go "Phwoarrr!" when they see me, but if you look closer you'll see that – on a good day – the positive outweighs the negative.

For example, I like my hair because it's long and thick and wavy and a really dark mahogany colour, but I hate my eyes, which are deep-set and surrounded by dark circles – I think they're piggy. I like my big pouty mouth and straight teeth, but hate my nose because it's too long and thin and pointy. I don't mind the top half of my body because I've got boobs and a waist, but my bottom half's a disaster with a lardy bum and big feet. Talking of feet, I could do with adding a few inches to my height, being only 5'2" and the shortest person I know.

Beth once said I looked like Helena Bonham Carter, which was very kind but, I think, completely untrue. Mind you, she thought I was taking the mickey when I once suggested she enter a modelling competition, so I know I'm not the only one who can be insecure about their looks. And since neither of us did too badly in the pulling stakes, we couldn't be that gross. Either that or the boys around our way were desperate.

Beth jolted me out of my thoughtful ponderings.

"Come on, you vain cow! Stop preening and let's get going," she grinned as she headed for the door. We both laughed as I struck my best Naomi Campbell pose and sashayed my way along an imaginary catwalk towards her.

"You know, I've got a funny feeling about tonight," she added as we headed down the stairs and into bright sunshine outside. "I reckon it's either going to be a complete disaster or we're both going to meet the guy of our dreams."

If I'd known she was going to be right on both counts, I would have stayed at home.

By the time we'd made the short walk into town, the atmosphere there was buzzing with anticipation. It was a hot, muggy summer's evening, with great grey thunderclouds bumbling on to the scene at high speed. The airless quality seemed to heighten the sizzle of expectation coming from the crowd of a hundred or so people gathered in the high street. Barriers had been erected between the road and pavement on both sides of the street and running along its entire length. Behind these great steel obstructions people stood five or six deep, their eyes focused intently on the entrance to the Style Café, waiting for something to happen.

The entrance itself had been roped off and three big doormen in dinner suits stood in front of the open doors and looked disparagingly at anyone who dared come near them. There was a bottleneck of people here, all crammed up against the barriers with cameras and autograph books in their hands, hoping to get a good look at anyone famous who happened to show up. The local TV station was here too, with a camera crew and interviewer standing on the highest of the three steps leading into the Café, waiting to pounce on anyone looking vaguely important.

I had a surreal feeling walking down the middle of the road towards the centre of activity, gold-coloured invitation clutched tightly in my hand. I felt like I'd walked on to a film set where Beth and I were the stars. Eyes bored into us as we made our way towards the entrance. The expressions on people's faces said it all: Who the hell are they? We didn't care, relishing the opportunity to strut our stuff, pretending to be divas if only for a few moments. At best we could hope to fool a few people into thinking we were minor *Neighbours* starlets, who'd maybe left the series six months ago and disappeared into provincial pantomime semi-oblivion. Actually, it didn't really matter that we were nobodies – I was having the time of my life. Some people were actually taking our photograph as we walked by! This was a hoot.

I spotted a few familiar faces from our college in the throng, gawping at us, clearly shocked. Much as I tried to suppress it, I couldn't contain the smirk that was spreading all over my face as I swaggered by. We breezed up to the doormen, handed over our tickets with a great flourish, stepped past them and went inside.

"This is *so* cool!" I breathed as I gazed at the scene in front of me. The decor was very modern, with primary coloured walls and acres of chrome. Miniature jukeboxes were placed on every table, while the bar swept along in a curve the whole length of the room. Beautiful people stood around in real designer clothes, the women fabulously made up and frighteningly long and skinny, the men taut, toned, tanned and tall. I felt like a munchkin next to them.

A waiter approached and offered us champagne from the tray he was carrying. We snatched greedily at a couple of glasses and began gulping the dry, impossibly fizzy stuff, spluttering as the bubbles hit the back of our throats and went up our noses. This wasn't your Asti Spumante rubbish, it was the real thing.

We threaded our way slowly through the throng of people, drinking in the atmosphere, light-headed from two sips of champagne. We sat down at a table and took it all in, only speaking when we saw someone we recognized from the telly or magazines. There was Vanya, international model, *Vogue* cover girl, and one of the patrons of the place, talking to a business type in a suit, and there was India, another model who was also an MTV presenter. It seemed the entire cast of every soap opera on the telly was here, and as my eyes roved about the room I noticed various deeply unattractive Premier division footballers wandering around the place and chatting up anything in a skirt.

And then I saw him.

He was propped up against the bar, taking

slug after slug from a bottle of beer while casually surveying everything going on around him. He looked like an Italian football star, with his short black wavy hair and smooth, tanned skin the colour of conker. His features were strong – a square jaw, sculptured cheek-bones, and deep-set eyes, dark as jet. He seemed totally at ease with himself standing there alone, one leg crossed casually over the other, and resting an elbow on the bar top. Gorgeous!

I decided he had to be a model, he looked so cool and confident. He certainly had the looks and the height (at a guess six foot of long, lean, loose limbs) and the clothes (black leather jeans, white T-shirt, black leather jacket). And he had that sort of "You can look but don't touch" air that models have about them. I was in lust.

About a millisecond later Beth saw him too.

"Oh! Wow!" The two words were separated by a long intake of breath so that the wow came out all elongated in a dramatic sigh of approval. She nudged me in the ribs with her elbow.

"Mel! Look," she hissed. "Can you see him? He's just . . . beautiful. Have you ever seen anyone so snoggable in your life?" Beth's eyes were like saucers as she turned to me, mouth gaping, face agog.

I stayed cool. "Hmm, nice bum, but not really

my type," I lied. Inside, my stomach went from swinging a merry dance of joy around and about my insides, to landing with a dull thud in the pit of my intestines. I was gutted. Oh well, might as well forget about him, I thought ruefully. I've got no chance now Beth's got wind of him.

I looked towards my friend, sitting there bolt upright and practically salivating in eager anticipation, and came to the conclusion that there were good and bad things about having a best friend who was an absolute babe. The best thing was that guys tended to swarm around you when you were in her company, thus boosting your ego and enabling you to flirt outrageously with some seriously fit lads. The downside was that your Best Friend The Babe always got to pick the choicest cut of prime beefsteak, which meant she'd go for the nice juicy piece of rump, while you ended up with the tripe.

Over the years of our friendship, I'd come to realize that our taste in guys was frighteningly similar, but that their taste in girls was completely unanimous, i.e. they all fancied Beth. That was why I'd developed my bog-standard "not my type" reply when she homed in on a guy and asked my opinion. I mean, a girl can only take so much rejection and there was no way I was going to get into a bitchy cat fight over a guy, because I knew our friendship was worth more than that. So I always backed down, gracefully letting my friend play tonsil hockey with some juicy-lipped hunk or other. And when, several minutes/days/weeks (delete as applicable) later, she invariably realized what a jerk he was, I thanked my lucky stars it wasn't me and comforted her in her few seconds of sorrow.

We sat in silence, surveying the vision in front of us. He must have sensed our eyes boring into him, devouring every centimetre of flesh, because he looked over in our direction and gave a huge, friendly smile, before looking away again.

We must have looked a right pair of plonkers as our two perfectly synchronized cheesy grins leered back at him!

Beth was the first to speak, choosing to do so out of the corner of her mouth so as not to raise his suspicions that we might be talking about him. Even though it meant her words coming out all muffled and sounding like she'd just had a tooth filled and the anaesthetic hadn't yet worn off.

"Did you see him? Did you see him smile at us?" Her words were urgent, as though she thought she'd perhaps imagined it and wanted reassurance that the love god had deigned to acknowledge our humble presence.

"Yes, Beth, I saw him," I said, "but can we hit the reality button for a second here? Because with looks like that, he's bound to (a) be a model, and (b) have a girlfriend. No, worse than that, I bet he's got four on the go and none of them will know anything about the others. Someone like that just has to be trouble. He's too perfect. Either that or he'll have a brain the size of a pea. Or he'll be an escaped psychopath. I mean, no one can be good looking and intelligent *and* a nice person, can they?"

"God, you're such a cynic!" Beth snorted in disgust. "You've got him all wrong. I reckon he's one of those types who doesn't realize how attractive he is. Kind of unassuming and shy. He'll have suffered a broken heart at an early age and he's wary of girls and needs to be brought out of himself a bit and shown what true love really is."

I pretended to stick my fingers down my throat and made loud gagging noises at the complete rubbish Beth was spouting, but she was getting into her stride now, and continued her deranged ramblings.

"Yeah, he'll have been totally in love. They were childhood sweethearts or something, and then she dumped him for a dirty old man with loads of dosh, and he's so hurt he's contemplating becoming a monk. Fortunately I'm here to save him from a life in brown frocks and purgatory. What do you think?"

"I think we'll find out soon enough," I answered. "He's coming over."

"Ohmigod! Why didn't you say anything before?" she hissed. "Have I got lipstick on my teeth?"

I shook my head and watched as Beth put on the performance of her life. Tossing her mane of hair, she drew her body up a couple more centimetres from the waist, arched her back (we'd read in a magazine that if you did this in front of a guy it was supposed to be very seductive, throwing him into a frenzy of uncontrollable passion or something) and thrust out her non-existent chest. Then she lifted one hand to her chin and began trailing it down her throat to her neck and chest, where she let it sit lightly for a moment, fiddling with her gold chain, and thus ensuring that any male looking in her direction would have his eyes popping out of his head.

I burst out laughing. Beth's man-eating techniques never failed to crack me up, but it was amazing how many lads fell for it, in spite of the over-the-top signals.

Taking a quick sideways glance at his

approaching body, she turned to me, her face lit up like a beacon, eyes wide and sparkling.

"You jammy cow, Mel," she hissed. "It's you he's got the hots for! I swear to God, I just looked at him and he didn't even see me. He's only got eyes for you." Beth hooted with laughter, relaxed back into her chair and grinned, a look of "Let's see what you're made of now, girl" on her face.

I was gobsmacked — not at Beth's reaction, because I knew that if push came to shove neither of us would stand in the other's way if a guy made a play for one of us. I was just stunned that, if she was right, someone so drop-dead gorgeous would be looking at me rather than any one of the other infinitely more stunning females in the room.

I glanced in his direction and saw that he was indeed looking directly at me, and smiling. I smiled back. It was an automatic reaction and about the only thing I could do. I certainly wasn't able to breathe or speak or move. My eyes were fixed on his so that I felt like an animal trapped in the headlights of an oncoming car. I suddenly developed a nervous tic to the side of one eye and could feel it twitching faster than a rabbit's nose. Convinced it was throbbing like a good 'un I wished I had Beth's cool attitude to guys, rather than getting in a fluster as I invariably did.

"Hi!" he said once he'd got close enough for me to smell his cologne. "Don't I know you from somewhere?"

Crikey! I wish! I thought, but there was no way I'd forget a face like that. So was that a line he was using, or had he genuinely mistaken me for someone else? Did it matter? Not likely! He's here now and all I have to do is be witty and entertaining and keep him interested and I might be in with a chance. I pulled myself together.

"Don't think so," I said and gave him my most winning smile. "I'm Mel and this is Beth," I carried on, gesticulating to my friend who just sat there grinning. Stuck for what to say next, I blurted out, "So, are you a model?" and nearly slit my throat at the crassness of the question. It is *so* uncool to ask someone that, I thought, and cringed visibly. Before he could run off laughing hysterically at my naff chat-up line, Beth saved me from further humiliation by asking him to join us, which he did, parking himself in the chair next to me.

"I'm Josh," he said. "Good party, isn't it?"

From then on the conversation went like a dream. He was so easy to chat to, and once I'd gathered myself back together after my opening *faux pas*, the three of us had a right laugh. It turned out that he wasn't a model, he was a mechanic, and that he knew someone who'd fitted out the inside of the Café, which was how he'd blagged a ticket. He was waiting for the same friend to turn up, but as they hadn't yet, and as he didn't know another soul there, he'd made up the story about knowing me as an excuse to talk to us, because we looked like "a laugh".

I kept finding my eyes drawn to his mouth as he talked. His lips were soft and plump and they turned up at the corners, giving his face an approachable look. He laughed a lot, a big throaty guffaw that showed off perfect white teeth and the cutest dimples in his cheeks. He gave out an aura that was confident without being arrogant, friendly but not overly so. And there was something inexplicably sexy about the way he put the beer bottle to his lips and took a glug from it. How I wished I was the mouth of that bottle!

He was divine.

I tried desperately to read his mind, to decode any subtle body language that might be going on, so that I could work out if he was making a play for either of us, but it was impossible. He seemed to make eye contact with us both equally, to chat just as much to one as the other. There were no clear signals that he fancied either of us, and I began to think that maybe he was the sort of friendly guy who would talk to anyone in complete innocence, not realizing the devastating effect he was having on them.

After a while he looked at his watch and said he was leaving. His mate obviously wasn't coming, and he had some things to "sort out" before the morning. As he stood up to leave, he turned to Beth, smiled, and said, "So, do you fancy going out somewhere tomorrow night?"

My heart shattered into a million pieces.

Chapter 2

You ungracious moo! I told myself later that night as I sat in front of my dressing-table mirror and scraped my make-up off. I mean, it's not as if you honestly expected him to fancy you, is it? So why the face-ache when he asked Beth out? Look at how pleased she was for you when she thought it was you he fancied!

I'd been tearing myself apart like this ever since Josh had got up and left us a few hours earlier. Beth could hardly contain her excitement at the prospect of a date with him. As she'd already heard me deny fancying him myself, it automatically gave her the go-ahead to say yes (and who in their right mind wouldn't?) and she spent the rest of the evening on cloud nine.

Meantime, my mood went from elation to

deflation in the space of about three seconds. I lost all desire to hunt out any other male talent, and just wanted to go home where I knew I could wallow in my own self-pity.

Beth tried to chivvy me along, pointing out fit guys at the party and suggesting we go and chat them up, but my heart wasn't in it. I knew she was trying hard to find me a lad so we could both go home on the high that you get when you've had a successful evening out on the pull, but I wasn't having any of it. Eventually, feeling a bit guilty for my bad mood, I gamely brought the conversation round to the topic I knew she was dying to discuss: her impending date with Josh. Beth rattled on, planning what she would wear and ruminating on where they might go, what they'd talk about, what sort of snogger he was, etc. And I sat and nodded, smiling vacantly, desperately trying to sum up more enthusiasm for the conversation than I felt, but wishing in my heart that I was in her shoes, that I was the one worrying about which outfit I'd wear for my hot date. Sadly, it wasn't to be.

Not even the sight of tasty Tony Harwood, the United goalkeeper and one of the fanciable faces I used to have stuck on my bedroom wall, could drag me from my bleak mood. Probably because he spent most of the evening at the bar chatting up a girl with legs up to her armpits and who was so top-heavy you felt she was going to fall flat on her face at any minute, which somehow seemed to depress me even more.

My mood was one of restless reflection when I went to bed that night and it took a lot of soul-searching before it dawned on me that, for the first time in my life, I was jealous of Beth. Not because the guy I fancied had asked her out instead of me – that had happened loads of times. No, I supposed it had something to do with the fact that throughout the entire time we'd spent with Josh, right from when he gave me that sexy look as he first walked over to us, I really thought I might be in with a chance, which didn't happen often when I was out with Beth.

So to go through all that, only to look on helplessly as he asked her out at the end of the evening, had caused a serious blow to my confidence. It made me acutely aware and – much as I hated to admit it – envious of the drop-dead gorgeous looks and chattily cheerful manner of my best friend.

I also felt a little unnerved by Beth's reaction to Josh. I'd never seen her quite so thrilled or animated about the prospect of a date with a guy. She got asked out so often it would be odd for a night out to pass by *without* anyone trying to hit on her, so I was used to her reaction to a lad's advances. Usually she'd be pleased to be chatted up, but she didn't normally go on and on about a first date with a guy, not like she had about Josh.

Both Beth and I had had relationships, but never anyone serious who we could imagine living with, or marrying even. And although we weren't puritanical, neither of us had experienced true love, and we'd certainly never had our hearts broken. We were too young and reckless to get involved. Or so I thought.

It was almost midday when I woke up. There must have been some kind of telepathy between me and Beth because, almost immediately, she rang.

"Hi! I just called to see how you were." Her voice sounded concerned.

"I'm fine. I think. I've only just got up. Took ages to get to sleep."

"Yeah, me too," she said. "I kept thinking about the evening. I must have been a real bore, rabbiting on about Josh, but I was so totally thrilled when he asked me out, it threw me into a bit of a panic. And then you seemed to go all quiet on me, so I thought I'd ring to see if everything was OK. I mean, I know you said you weren't interested in him, but . . . well, I wanted to check. I don't want to hurt your feelings or stand in your way or anything."

I felt like such a git. There I was harbouring all these horribly envious thoughts about my best friend, and she was the one being completely magnanimous and lovely and caring. Like best friends should be. Unlike me, who was being a total cow. I had to make amends.

"No, no, it's OK, he's really not my type," I said, forcing an upbeat into my voice. Then I added, "Anyway, I've been thinking too and I reckon Josh is a really nice guy and you ought to go for it. He's obviously well into you, he's totally amazing-looking and seems really caring, and you deserve to go out with someone decent. You're made for each other – you'll probably end up getting married, living in a big house, and having a rugby team of kids together."

"Whoa! Hang on a second," she laughed. "I'd settle for a snog at the moment. But he *is* very cute, so I'm not ruling out the big wedding. Will you be bridesmaid?"

"Only if you promise I can wear a big frothy pink number, so I look like a meringue. *Not.* Will you be marrying in white as a sign of your purity? Actually, I think I can answer that. Definitely not."

She laughed. "Scarlet will be much more appropriate. Something by Jean Paul Gaultier, very tight and revealing and Madonna-esque. Something that'll give a few aged aunts heart palpitations, not to mention the vicar. And we'll have a huge marquee on the lawn of our country house, and eat smoked salmon and strawberries and cream and drink gallons of the poshest champagne."

"I've never wanted to get married in a church," I mused. "I fancy doing it in a castle on a remote island in the Outer Hebrides. Or in Transylvania. I'll wear black antique lace and we'll have a huge medieval banquet with pigs roasting on a spit and mulled wine and court jesters. And our honeymoon suite will have a massive four-poster bed with a velvet bedspread and fresh flowers strewn all over the room. We'll have our own personal butler who'll wait on us so that we don't have to leave the bedroom ever again."

"Saucy! So do you have anyone in mind for this sumptuous event?" Beth asked.

I thought for a moment before answering. "I think it's between Leonardo di Caprio and the lad in the cola advert on the telly at the moment. Either of them would do. I'm not too fussy."

"Says the girl who turned down Ollie Wilson,

just about the cutest guy on our course and who's madly in lust with you!" cried Beth. "You've got to be the pickiest person I've ever met."

"Yeah, but come on! Ollie Wilson has been out with virtually every girl in college. The only reason he hasn't asked *you* out is because even he knows his limitations. And I'm not interested in soiled goods. Anyway, you're the one with the guy of your dreams banging on your door, so it's you we'll talk about. What will you be called when you marry Josh? Mrs Bethany what?"

She giggled. "Actually, I'll have to pass on that one. I haven't a clue what his surname is. And yet here I am hearing wedding bells. Sad or what? Shall we change the subject?"

"Mmm. Are we still on for Bradbury on the 26th?"

"Oh wow! Yes!" Beth shouted. "I'm really excited about that, almost as much as getting my hands on Josh."

Bradbury was one of the highlights of the year. It was a massive music festival held over two days in the middle of summer. All the hippest bands would be playing, and it had become an annual pilgrimage for around seventy thousand young people into music and having a good time. Last year was the first time we'd managed to persuade our parents to let us go for a day. This year they'd agreed to let us take my dad's smelly old tent from his days as a boy scout and camp overnight. I could hardly wait.

We spent the next few minutes making vague arrangements about our trip and I came off the phone feeling heaps better. No guy was worth bitterness between friends and I knew the relationship I had with Beth would outlast any boyfriend either of us might have. Josh wasn't the guy of my dreams, however much I might have thought so last night. He was a fleeting fantasy and Beth was welcome to him.

I think I could have got on with my Josh-less life if it wasn't for the fact that during the next week Beth went out with him about every other night and first thing next morning would call me to give me a second-by-second account of each date in the most gruesome detail. I therefore felt like I knew him better than his own mother. I knew that his favourite pizza topping was ham and pepperoni with a fried egg in the middle (ugh!); that the little finger of his left hand was permanently crooked from a bicycle accident when he was nine years old; that he had a tattoo of a raging bull on his left arm; and that he was the most fabulous snogger Beth had ever come across. I could go on.

Matters weren't helped by the fact that Beth and I were in the middle of our summer break from college, which meant that we both had time on our hands, much of which was spent discussing guys (like you do) and more to the point, Josh. When we weren't talking about him, we were seeing him, as he became increasingly included in our social scene and I felt more and more like a gooseberry. This was entirely my fault, as I was the one who sometimes suggested he come out with us, because I knew it meant I got to see more of him. And, without trying to sound too contradictory, I really didn't mind Josh being around, but at the same time I did.

You see, whenever I went out with Josh and Beth and whoever else happened to come along, I spent most of my time lusting quietly in a corner, watching him on the sly, studying his every move. I'd sit there, wishing I was in Beth's shoes when he put his arm round her shoulder, or kissed her tenderly on the lips, or brushed a few stray blonde hairs away from her eyes. I spent most of my time fantasizing about him, soaking him up, putting myself in Beth's place.

At other times I resented his presence. It felt like he was muscling in on our friendship, changing the dynamics of our relationship. Whenever we went out as a threesome, the conversations we had were totally different from those Beth and I had on our own. There was no ogling of other lads, no light-hearted bitching sessions at other people's expense, no detailed chats about the shade of nail varnish we were wearing. I felt I had to behave in a more grown-up manner, be more mature than I was when it was just me and Beth. Consequently, I tried to work it so that Beth and I would get together at least a couple of times a week, just so we could catch up on girls-only gossip.

I had decided that Bradbury was going to be one occasion that was definitely Josh-free. It was an event that had been in our diaries long before he came on the scene, and, after the blast we'd had together there last year, I was determined to relive the experience. I'd spent weeks deciding what to take to wear, eat, drink, etc. and by the time I'd arranged to call round to Beth's house the day before we were due to go to finalize the details for the trip, I was packed and raring to go. I was just about to leave when she rang. Her voice sounded husky, her tone down.

"I can't come," she wailed. "I've got the flu. I'm really sorry."

Poor Beth, I truly felt for her. I knew she was

looking forward to going as much as me, so she must be feeling rough to have to pull out. I tried to comfort her.

"Oh no! That's such bad luck," I commiserated. "You don't think you'll feel any better by the morning, if you get an early night and hit the Lemsip?"

Beth said no, that the symptoms had only developed overnight and that she felt like she was going to die. "Will you still go?" she wailed.

"No," I answered, "not by myself. It wouldn't be the same. Don't worry though, we'll go next year." I made a few more feeble attempts at consoling her, then ordered her back to bed and put the phone down, thoroughly disappointed.

Then a thought struck me: why on earth *shouldn't* I go on my own? There was no reason in the world not to. OK, so it wouldn't be the same as going with Beth, but it would be a bit of an adventure.

There was just one small snag: my parents. They wouldn't let me camp out on my own. Mind you, I had no desire to do that either – there were too many weirdos about. However, the majority of my favourite bands were playing on the Sunday anyway, and they might agree to me going for the day if I caught them in a good mood.

Dad could be a bit of a fossil, but Mum was quite cool sometimes. I'd ask Mum. And I'd tell her Beth wasn't going but I was meeting Dee Barrett. Mum approved of Dee – she liked the fact that she was smart and sensible and was going to be an accountant. Dee was going with a bunch of kids from her Advanced Maths course, so I could make a loose arrangement with her and tell Mum it was definite. Then if I did feel like meeting people I could, but if I felt like an adventure (which at this moment I did) then I could do that too. Perfect.

It was midday when I arrived at Gate 9, one of the many entrances to the festival. My parents had been surprisingly easygoing about the situation, only insisting that I take Dad's mobile phone and call them if I needed to. I think they were placated by the fact that I wasn't disappearing to the other side of the country, or hitch-hiking, or anything dumb like that.

Bradbury was a village only twenty miles from where we lived and I'd caught the train and then a special bus laid on for the event which ferried passengers to the site – a huge field a couple of miles out of the village. I'd spoken to Dee and said if I wasn't at Gate 9 by 11.30 a.m., to go on without me.

I didn't make it.

The sun was beating down from high in the sky, offset by a breeze that was cooling on my face and bare arms. I was humming a tune as I sauntered along, taking in the surroundings, listening to snatches of conversation from the ever-increasing throng of festival-goers all around me. As I got closer to the main stage, the throng became a mass, while the conversation became a cacophony of sound and music. There was a really good feeling in the air. Complete strangers smiled at each other, said hello, shared drinks and food. I felt totally at ease on my own, like I was melting into the crowd, visible yet inconspicuous.

Although I was having a good time, I did feel awfully sorry for Beth – she was missing a great day. I'd considered ringing her to see if she'd made a quick enough recovery and to tell her I was going anyway, but came to the conclusion that it would make her feel even more miserable if she couldn't make it. So I didn't. Anyway, I felt sure she'd have called me if she was up to going.

I headed for the same spot Beth and I had discovered last year, where you could get a good view of the main stage, see one of the big screens transmitting the event in close-up, but not get completely squashed like the people in the front third of the crowd. There was enough room to move around and dance, and even sit down if you wanted to be really unsociable or needed to chill out from freaking out to the music.

I walked towards the funnel of bodies packed in tight at the front of the stage then stopped dead, all the breath knocked out of me. I stared at the figure who'd just walked in front of me. Was it? No, it couldn't be. Hang on, the head's turning this way a little. *Yes, it is! It's Josh!* I was dumbfounded. I'd never expected to see anyone I knew in a crowd of this size, let alone Josh. *It must be fate.*

All the thoughts and feelings I'd been shoving to a closed corner at the back of my brain over the past few weeks came gushing to the fore again. My emotions soared to a new high of elation at the sight of him. He looked even more gorgeous, more tanned, and more cool than I remembered. He was wearing one of those T-shirts that are tight across the chest and arms, emphasizing each rippling muscle and his perfectly chiselled pecs. I could just make out the outline of the bottom half of the raging bull tattoo Beth had told me about on his left arm. I had an overwhelming desire to kiss it. My heart was drowning out the sound of the music playing, thrashing out its own message, demanding some kind of reciprocation for its urgent beat. *This isn't a childish little fantasy*, I thought. *This is love.*

I began walking again, keen not to lose him in the horde of people, but not daring to get close enough so that he might catch me spying on him. He was carrying burgers and Cokes, threading his way carefully through the crowd so as not to drop anything.

If he's here with a bunch of guys I'll talk to him, I decided. If he's with a girl, I'll disappear into the mêlée and pray to God that I haven't caught him two-timing Beth. I didn't have long to find out. Stretching out both arms, he threw them around a girl in the crowd in front of him, kissing her on the cheek, then the neck, then the shoulders. I could see quite clearly who he was with.

It was Beth.

Chapter 3

"You rotten schemer!" I seethed. "You conniving, lying, rotten. . ." I could hardly contain my anger as I stood there, cemented to the spot, watching my best friend canoodling with her boyfriend, totally unaware of my presence. Not only that but she looked a picture of glowing health and vitality, instead of confined to her sickbed with the most horrific attack of flu known to mankind.

What the hell was Beth playing at? To my mind, it didn't take much working out. If I was being hugely generous I could say that her illness had taken a very sudden turn for the better and that she'd felt well enough to come to Bradbury. But if that was the case, why hadn't she called me? She knew how desperate I was to be here.

No, the truth was obvious. Beth would rather be here with Josh than here with me. She'd chosen her boyfriend of a few weeks over her friend of twelve years.

I suddenly felt all alone in that crowd of seventy thousand people. The babble of noise around me became a faint drone in the background, drowned out by the rapid-fire thought processes screaming through my head. She must have planned it all, I thought bitterly – told me bare-faced lies and betrayed our friendship.

I felt so angry I could have gone up to her right then and slapped her in the face. But no, however much that would make me feel better, it would have been a childish reaction and ultimately one I'd regret. I needed to be a bit more mature about this, to sort it out in my own head before I confronted her, which I would do when the time was right.

I turned on my heels and fled, my solo adventure in ruins. The prospect of seeing top bands play paled into complete insignificance against what had just happened. As I trudged along in despair, my emotions began to change from anger to hurt. I felt a niggling ache gnawing at my insides, as though I'd suffered a major loss or had a limb torn off or something equally traumatic. Well, this *was* traumatic. Was that it?

I wondered. Was our friendship over now? Could it survive such treachery?

I became consumed with jealousy. I felt Josh was my great rival, that we were fighting for Beth's attention, and that her loyalty to me was being passed over to him instead. I felt he was beginning to take my place in her affections, that soon I would be redundant, dumped on the scrap heap of life. Worse, I was jealous of Beth too, for having Josh when I didn't. I had no one. And, much as I hated to admit it, part of me wished that it was me there with Josh, that I was the one whose cheek he was kissing, not Beth.

As I walked the hurt subsided and I began to put things into perspective. Yes, it was terrible of Beth to choose Josh instead of me, but likewise it was pathetic of me to be resentful because he preferred her. Was that what was at the core of all this? Pure jealousy? And if that's all it was, could our friendship stand such a test? Damn! How I wished we'd never met Josh.

I made my way home feeling unloved, unwanted, pitiful and confused.

I left it until the next day before I rang Beth, which gave me the chance to make some sense of my mixed-up thoughts. Just.

Her mum answered, and shouted for Beth to

come to the phone. She seemed to take for ever, while I sat there, chewing my nails and thinking, "If she puts on a pathetic, weedy voice and claims that she's still feeling rough, I'm going to hit the roof."

The voice which greeted me, however, was plainly nowhere near death's door.

"Hi! How are you?" she chirruped brightly.

"I'm fine, thanks. More importantly, how are you?"

"Much better actually. It must have been one of those twenty-four-hour bugs. In fact. . ." She paused for a second, as though gathering her thoughts together, then added, ". . .I feel a bit guilty. I went to Bradbury all day yesterday after all. I called you a couple of times to see if we could meet but there was no reply, so I figured you were all out. Or whatever. You know, Mel, you really need to get your family into the Nineties and get yourselves an answering machine."

An instant wave of relief swept over me, quickly followed by guilt – relief that she had tried to contact me after all and guilt for the unspeakable judgements I'd made in the past few hours, based solely on my overactive imagination rather than hard facts. Was I glad I hadn't smacked her at the festival!

"Oh. Right. So how was it? Did you go on your own?" I was thinking hard. I couldn't admit that I too had been to Bradbury but had stormed off in a fit of childish jealousy when I saw her with Josh. I'd have to pretend I'd spent the day knitting or something.

"No. I called up Josh, and luckily for me he was at a loose end. The whole day was absolutely fantastic, but I'm not going to rattle on about it or you'll be sick with envy."

I insisted that Beth did indeed rattle on, and we chatted for ages – until my mum shouted that I had to pay for the next phone bill, and we rang off.

Then, as much out of curiosity as anything else, I dialled 1471, the British Telecom service that gives you the number of the last person who called and also the time they rang. To me the service was a toy I'd be forever grateful to the telephone company for. I used the service quite often, usually when I was hoping a particularly hunky boy would ring. Gone were the days of sitting in by the phone like a sad old sausage, waiting for him to call. At least now you could go out for an hour or so and – unless your phone rings non-stop – be able to work out if he'd tried to get in touch.

The voice at the end of the line was austere,

the message final. It told me that the last incoming call to the house was made two days previously, and it wasn't Beth's number. Beth had said she'd phoned me yesterday morning.

She was lying.

Beth and I had been friends for a long time, since we were five years old. Nothing had ever come between us before. In all those years we'd never had a fight or a row – we rarely disagreed, even. We were like two tennis players in a doubles match, complementing each other perfectly, playing as a team. We'd been through a lot together, sharing all our experiences. Nothing was sacred, and I felt I knew as much about Beth as anyone did, and vice versa. She was like a sister and mother and best friend all rolled into one. My life would be empty without her.

And now...? And now I felt like my whole world was falling apart, and I was as much to blame for it as anyone.

It was a day later and I had come to the conclusion that I had to sort out this web of lies – mine as well as Beth's – once and for all. I took the short bus journey to her house and knocked on her front door. It took an age for her to answer but when she did, as always she looked delighted to see me – until she saw the serious look on my face. Then her face turned from a bright smile to one of quizzical concern.

"We need to talk," I said. "We've got a lot to discuss. Is anyone else at home?"

"Er, no. What's up? You look like you've been up all night. What's happened?"

She stood aside to let me in and I headed for the sitting-room.

"I *have* been up all night," I replied. "I've been up all night trying to work out how to say this to you, trying to sort out in my head what's been going on."

"Wh-wh-what do you mean? What have I done?" Her face was scrunched up now into a look of confusion mixed with fear – the fear of what I was going to say next. I could see it in her eyes. The penny had dropped. She knew I'd found out, she knew why I was here.

"Look, Beth," I said in an almost matronly manner, "I know you lied to me. I know you were at Bradbury because I saw you there. With Josh. I decided to go on my own. I thought it would be like some stupid Indiana Jones adventure. And when I saw you I was livid. I thought you'd planned it all because you wanted to be there with him, not me.

"Then when you gave me all that spiel about phoning me, about how you really wanted me to be there with you, I felt like such a git because, believe me, I'd harboured some pretty rotten thoughts about you. But now I know you didn't call at all. That it was a load of crap. So I decided right, I'm going to get to the bottom of this, and that's why I'm here."

I looked at her, trying to gauge her reaction. Was she going to try and lie her way out of it or come clean? I didn't have to wait too long to find out. Her face crumpled, her bottom lip and chin began quivering, and her eyes welled up, a lake of tears.

"I . . . er . . . I'm really s-s-sorry," she wailed. Then she slumped into a sofa, covered her face with her hands and sat there howling.

"I f-f-eel like s-s-such a fraud!" she said, between great heaving gasps of breath. "I knew I shouldn't have g-gone with him. I know you w-w-won't believe this, but I said we ought to phone you, b-but Josh wanted it to be just me and h-him." She took a huge gulp of air and let out a long breath in an attempt to control herself. Then she looked up at me through weepy eyes and carried on.

"I *was* ill," she said, wiping her eyes with the back of her hand. "Honestly. And I did feel better on Saturday. But Josh phoned me and kept going on and on about wanting us to go together. I'd told him you and I had planned to go months ago, before he was around, but he still kept nagging me.

"And then I thought it wouldn't matter because you'd have called me if you'd changed your mind and were going to go anyway, and I thought you'd have arranged to do something else by then if you weren't. So . . . so I went with Josh instead. And I suppose you're right, I *did* want to be with him. Which makes me feel even worse." Her bottom lip started to wobble again as she went on. "And I lied to you because I felt guilty and it just came out and I'm really, really sorry."

By this time I'd sat down next to her, my hands clasped, staring at my thumbnails. It was time for me to unburden myself too.

"Look," I said, "to be honest with you, I'm probably overreacting. You see, the truth is I'm as jealous as hell of you and Josh. And when I saw you together yesterday, I flipped. It brought everything I've been feeling over the past few weeks to a head. I keep having visions of him taking up more of your life, and you wanting to be with him rather than me. I keep thinking that he's somehow going to come between us, that there isn't enough room in your life for me and him, and that he'll somehow break up our friendship and take my place. Which is dumb, I know, but there you go."

I gave her a weak smile and raised my eyes to the heavens in dramatic fashion.

She looked completely taken aback. "You're crazy!" she scolded. "As if he could take your place. I mean, do you honestly think I could sit down with Josh and discuss in tiny detail what I'm going to wear to go out that night? Or expect him to watch me change outfits fifteen times in the space of three hours, just to go shopping? Or have a silly conversation about getting married? To him? He'd think I was mad!"

"But you *have* been spending a lot of time with him," I interjected.

Beth chewed on this notion for a moment, then frowned before saying, "You're right. But I've been so consumed with him that if you hadn't pointed it out, I probably wouldn't have realized. I'm sorry I've neglected you. I suppose the novelty of going out with a guy like Josh hasn't worn off yet. I'm being a bit besotted and pathetic really."

Then I carried on, to the much more painfully embarrassing bit. "Yeah, but it's not just that," I said, feeling my cheeks flush in readiness for the next confession. "The thing is, when we first saw Josh I fancied him something rotten too, even

45

though I told you I didn't . . . so at least we're quits on the lying front. I kind of had a feeling he'd fall for you, so I kept my mouth shut to save us the embarrassment of having to fight for him – and you losing." I laughed nervously at my attempt to make light of the situation. Thankfully, so did Beth.

"I mean, there's no getting away from it," I continued, "he's seriously tasty. And I would've been able to forget about him and go back to fancying footballers or pop stars if you didn't keep waffling on about him. You've been giving me a right old earache!"

"I know, I must have been really irritating," she grimaced. "I had a feeling you fancied him though – I could tell by the way you were looking at him. That's why I phoned you up the day after we met him at the Style Café."

"It doesn't matter now," I sighed. "None of this would have happened if I'd been totally straight with you from the start. So I'm the one who should be apologizing."

"Look, Mel," said Beth, taking hold of my hand in hers and giving it a comforting pat, "I can promise you with all my heart, this thing I've got with Josh won't change anything between you and me. We've known each other for most of our lives. I'm not going to chuck that away for a guy who'll probably dump me in a couple of weeks."

"It's odd," I said, thinking aloud, "but it's never bothered me before. We've both had lads on the go at one time or another and I've never felt threatened by them, and I bet you haven't either. It's almost as though they've always been a bit of fun in the past – a bit of frivolity to brighten up a dull day. But Josh is different. I expect it's because I can sense that maybe he's the one for you, so I'm feeling a bit insecure about it all."

She nodded vigorously. "I understand completely. I'd feel exactly the same if it was you falling head over heels for a guy. I'd be pig sick with worry that I was going to have my nose pushed out. And if you're worried about me fretting over the fact that you fancy Josh, forget it. *Everyone* fancies him. My *mum* fancies him! I'd be gutted if they didn't. I'm just pleased that my best friend has got such excellent taste!"

"You're so sweet," I said, tears pricking at the corners of my eyes. "I don't deserve a friend like you."

"Course you do," she grinned. "We deserve each other. What you need to do though, if you don't mind me dishing out advice, is get out there, get a boyfriend and fall in love, then we can all go out as a cosy foursome. Wouldn't that be great?"

Beth was absolutely right, and that was exactly what I intended to do.

Chapter 4

Once I'd made the conscious decision to stop swooning over the unobtainable, i.e. Josh, and, well, *get a life* (or at least a boyfriend), my head seemed to have cleared a little, turfing out the farcical notions and fantasies that had been cluttering it up and replacing them with a more realistic concept, which was to find a replacement for my affections.

This was a lot harder than I first thought. I thought that if I could just bring myself to snog lots of guys lots of times, then maybe one would take the place that Josh had been evicted from. But since meeting Josh, every other guy I came into contact with was immediately compared and contrasted with him. And very few seemed to stand up under scrutiny. They were either

(a) more immature than Josh, (b) less gorgeous than Josh, (c) sillier, geekier, not as temperature-raising as Josh, or (d) all of the above. And most of them came under category (d).

Just as I was about to resign myself to a life of celibacy, Nick re-entered my life. He had joined my General Studies class a month or so before we broke up for the summer holidays, being new to the area and part-way through a Business Studies course at his previous college. I'd noticed he was pretty fit-looking and had harboured some rather lustful fantasies about him over the weeks, but never thought he'd give me a second glance. Then college finished and along came Josh, so Nick had been shoved to the nether regions of my mind and forgotten about.

Then I bumped into him again (literally) in the Transport section of books in W H Smith – glamorous, eh? I was looking for a birthday present for my dad and, knowing his passion for cars, was making my way blindly round acres of books on the subject, looking completely flummoxed. He (Nick that is, not Dad) was engrossed in a book on Ferraris when I accidentally trod on his foot. It broke the ice (not to mention his toe, I thought later) and he helped me choose a book and then asked me if I'd like to go out sometime.

I was surprised at my reaction to the blinding

smile he gave me – the encounter was the nearest I'd got since Josh to making my heart skip a beat (it sort of limped a bit, nothing more). However, it didn't take much effort to say yes.

Understandably, on the afternoon of our date, the entire contents of my wardrobe were discarded as totally lacking in sophistication. I ended up whizzing into town and spending far too much money on a slinky black dress and high heels. As I took a bus to our rendezvous point, I felt ready for the Ritz, at the very least.

When I saw Nick, he was barely recognizable. As I watched him coming down the road towards me, I suddenly realized why he'd suggested we meet at The Roxy, the rather rundown 50s-style establishment that old farty aunts and uncles went to on a Saturday night in an attempt to relive their youth.

I thought we were meeting there because there was a particularly trendy bar just round the corner, but I soon realized my horrible mistake.

I saw the hair first. You couldn't miss it. His shoulder-length blond bob had been transformed – uplifted from the roots and built into a skyscraper of a quiff that went from the end of his nose to the nape of his neck and waggled about furiously as he walked. He wore a purple shiny shirt with lapels the size of plane wings, a black long-line jacket and green drainpipe trousers that were either too short or specially designed to show off the sparkly blue and silver socks and skinny white shins underneath. His shoes were pink, with thick black crêpe soles which added to his already giraffe-like height.

In the split second that it took to work out that yes-this-was-my-date-for-the-evening-and-I-wonder-if-I-can-do-a-runner-before-he-sees-me, it was too late.

"Hi, Mel!" he grinned, his hair bouncing towards me a good half an hour before he did. "Bet you didn't expect to see me like this, did you?"

"Um, no," I spluttered, "I didn't realize you were a 50s freak." I made sure I emphasized the word "freak", but the irony was lost on him.

"I get it from my old man. He's a DJ – loves the music, the clothes, the whole era. I guess it's rubbed off on me. Shall we go inside?"

No! the voice inside my head screamed. I do *not* want to go inside. I hate that sort of music, I can't dance to it, and I know I'll feel totally out of place in a roomful of *Grease* throwbacks. Get me out of here. Now!

"OK."

The voice speaking didn't belong to me – it was a masochistic alien living inside my body that had momentarily taken me over. I cursed it. I also cursed my complete lack of assertiveness as I meekly allowed him to lead me inside, like a lamb to the slaughter.

Not surprisingly, the evening was a disaster. Aside from the fact that the only thing we had in common was that we were both from planet Earth (just), there was something about the way he danced that made me want to be somewhere else. Anywhere else. I've always found it totally amazing how even if you fancy a lad something rotten, once he hits the dance floor, all thoughts of sharing a snog or two leap straight out of the window.

Guys who think they're dead cool, desperately serious dancers, but who in fact look like your Great Uncle Albert getting on down to *Saturday Night Fever* at your granny's Silver Wedding anniversary, are the worst. All illusions are shattered as they bump and grind in the most overtly sexual, yet hilariously off-putting manner. Nick was like that, only worse. He jiggled away furiously on the dance floor, totally convinced he was Danny Zucko grooving his way through *Summer Nights*. He looked more like Danny de Vito attempting the same moves.

I spent most of the evening trying to blend in with the walls, while avoiding going anywhere near the dance floor. At 11p.m. I made an excuse about having to be up early the next morning, and headed for the door.

"That was great," grinned Nick as he walked me to the nearest taxi rank. "We must do it again some time. What do you think?"

"Er, I'm not sure when – I'm about to go on holiday," I lied. "Give me your phone number and I'll call you when I get a minute." I felt a bit mean as he scribbled his number down on a piece of paper for me to lose as soon as he'd gone, but I honestly didn't think I could cope with another evening quite as challenging as that.

If I could thank Nick for anything it was that he was a turning-point in my life. For the first time since meeting Josh I had actually been out with another guy and, even though it had been a shambles, I felt like I was on the road to recovery.

Not long after, I met Danny. He seemed like a much better prospect all round. The way we got together was really corny, the sort of thing you see on the telly but never believe happens in real life.

It was a Saturday night and I was sitting indoors with nowhere to go and no one to go out with. I was feeling a bit sorry for myself because, I mean, no one of my age should be sitting in front of the telly watching pathetic quiz shows and the 29th showing of *Ghost* on the most popular going-out night of the week, should they? I imagined every other teenager in the entire universe out having a good time, and here I was, a channel-hopping couch potato. Even my parents had deserted me, off on one of their Rotary Club do's, although perhaps that was a good thing. I was in such a bad mood, I would only have been completely foul to them if they had been around.

I decided to indulge myself by watching old videos while stuffing my face and painting my nails.

I phoned for a Bellybusters pizza to be delivered – ham and pepperoni with extra anchovies. In the forty minutes that I had to wait I had a long soak in the bath, put on a strawberry and cucumber face mask, painted each fingernail an experimental different colour, and began watching the first series of *Friends* for the umpteenth time. The only trouble with that was whenever I laughed another huge crater appeared in the green mask that my face was hiding under.

Then the doorbell rang. It was my pizza delivery.

I stumbled into the hall in my Garfield slippers

and raggy dressing-gown and opened the front door, only to be met by an apparition of male loveliness, sporting black hair, black leathers and a ten-inch Bellybusters pizza box. He looked like a more clean-cut version of Josh.

"42 Ragdale Drive, name of Saunders?" he asked matter-of-factly.

"Hur, hur . . . huh. . ." I spluttered, not daring to open my mouth too wide to talk, for fear of my green mask cracking into even bigger crevices. Hours seemed to pass as he stared at the green alien from another planet standing at the door, while I peered back at the vision before me. "Mmm," I nodded, once the initial shock had worn off. "That's me."

He grinned. "You're at Missendon College, aren't you? I recognized the name. Tourism and Travel, isn't it?"

I was stunned. He was absolutely right about the college and the course, but I'd never seen him before in my life – though quite how I'd managed to miss him, I would never know.

"You hang out with that girl with the blonde hair . . . her name's Mel or something."

"Beth, she's called Beth. I'm Mel."

"Oh, right, that's it." He stood looking at me, as though waiting for me to continue the conversation. All I could do was think how ridiculous I looked, while kicking myself for slathering my face in this dumb face mask that would no doubt bring me out in spots or send me into an allergic reaction. I must have had a totally blank expression on my face, which he took to mean: conversation over.

"Er, anyway," he said quickly, "your pizza. £5.50, please."

He held out the box, which I took, unable to speak. Still mute, I handed him the money, and he turned to walk away.

Then my brain bounced back into gear. Hang on a minute! it whirred. Don't let him go. Keep him talking. What have you got to lose? Only pride when he laughs in my face, whined the negative half of my cranium. Tick, tick, tick. . .

"So . . . have you been working for Belly-busters long?" I managed in a strained voice.

"About three hours so far," he smiled. "This is my first night."

"Oh." My mind raced ahead of me, digging deep for another question to keep the conversation going.

"I don't suppose you get many nights to yourself in a job like that," I reasoned, not realizing quite how forward I was sounding. "It must be rotten for your social life."

"It's pretty grim, but I do get one night off a

week," he replied. "I'm not working on Monday night. Are you up to anything then?"

"Erm, no. . ." My voice tailed off.

"Would you like to go for a drink?"

I grinned. "I'd love to."

"Brilliant. Shall I pick you up at say, eight o'clock?"

"Excellent." I grinned again and my face mask cracked completely, small shards chipping off and flaking on to the collar of my dressing-gown. He laughed, a funny, slightly hysterical laugh, said he had to go because he had five other pizza deliveries in his bag, waved his leather-clad hand, and sauntered back down the path.

I slipped back inside the hallway, threw the pizza in the bin (who needs food when you're in heaven?) and went straight to my room, where I spent the rest of the night planning what I was going to wear.

Unfortunately, Danny turned up. I say unfortunately because he then proceeded to spend the entire evening asking me deeply probing questions about . . . Beth. Things like: "So, how did you and . . . um . . . Beth meet? And what's she like, as a . . . um . . . person? What are her favourite foods/films/music?" They were the kinds of questions a potential boyfriend should be asking about you, not your bloomin' drop-dead gorgeous best friend.

It took about ten minutes for me to work out that it wasn't me he was interested in at all, and that the line he'd used on Saturday night where he pretended not to be entirely sure of her name was complete garbage. The guy was obsessed with her!

I wasn't at all surprised when, halfway through the evening he suggested we (namely me, him and Beth) should go bowling together. Not ruddy likely! I thought. Yes, that would be lovely, I said, then added that I was starving and shouldn't we order some food? We did. I went for the most expensive nosh on the menu, then, midway through pudding I excused myself to go to the loo, nipped out through a side exit and went home. *Touché!*

It was Todd who finally put a stop to my attempts to forget Josh. He was an American student over here on a six-month exchange trip. He was stay-ing with a family my parents knew, and it was my mum (of all people) who set me up with him, thinking it would be nice for someone of his age to show him around town. Although I didn't fancy his bookish looks one iota, such was my determination to get on with my life *après* Josh that I agreed to go out with him, convincing myself I was doing my bit for Anglo-American relations.

He suggested we meet in the Style Café and a thousand and one memories came flooding back as I walked through the door. That was the bar where I had first laid eyes on Josh. Over there was the table we had all sat around, laughing and joking like we'd known each other all our lives.

I was there before Todd, so I ordered a Becks, the same beer Josh was drinking on that fateful night a lifetime ago, and stood, propped up at the bar, slugging straight from the bottle just like he had. Immediately realizing how ridiculous I was being, I shook myself back to reality, poured the sparkly golden liquid into a tall glass and sat down at the bar.

I was nervous – not at the thought of meeting Todd, but because I knew Josh often came here for a quick beer on his way home from work. The thought of seeing him again tied more knots in my stomach than a trawlerman's fishing net, and I sat hugging my glass and rubbing my sweating palms on my skirt in an effort to stay cool. One half of me prayed that he wouldn't walk in, the other half pleaded that he would.

Five-past eight. Todd was late. I was starting to feel a tad embarrassed sitting there on my own. I surveyed the room, and realized how out of place I must have looked – a sole person in a sea of couples, groups, or gangs of young people. No one else seemed to be alone.

I looked at my watch. Eight minutes past eight. Every minute was dragging by. One minute felt like twelve. I decided to give him half an hour. We did say eight, didn't we? And we did say we'd meet here, not somewhere else. Didn't we? I began to doubt myself. My mind searched for all possible explanations for Todd's non-arrival, and found none.

I looked at the funky chrome clock above the bar. Finally it read half-past eight. Right, that's it. I'm off. I'd obviously been stood up – and even if I hadn't, even if the wretched Todd just happened to have broken a leg falling off a bus on his way here, I wasn't hanging around in a bar on my own looking like a complete lemon *any longer*.

I grabbed my bag off the bar, and slipped off my stool as inconspicuously as possible, hoping no one would see me trying to slither out un-noticed. However, thanks to my own paranoia, I felt as though everyone's eyes were boring into me as I walked towards the door, and I imagined people sniggering and sneering at the girl whose boyfriend hadn't turned up. My eyes fixed firmly on the floor, my face red with the humiliation of it all, I stumbled out of the door and walked straight into Josh.

"Hey, what's up?" he chuckled, grabbing me by the shoulders as I buffeted my way into him. "You haven't been stood up, have you?" He grinned at me, obviously thinking he'd made quite a good joke. My humiliation turned to anger – a great defence mechanism when you're suddenly confronted by the guy of your dreams in an uncompromising situation. Not.

"No!" I spluttered indignantly. "I just had to call in to give someone a message. What's it to you, anyway?" My face must have been a furious shade of fuchsia because Josh backed away immediately, holding both hands up as though to say, "Whoa! What have I done to deserve this?"

I was even more flustered now. Having him hold me like that and being able to smell the delicious aroma of his body at such close quarters sent my mind into a spiral of confusion. I had just one thought: to get away.

I pushed past him and fled down the steps into the street. I didn't look back as I rushed away. I couldn't, or else he would have seen tears of anguish coursing down my cheeks.

I felt like such a fool. What must he have thought of me, blowing up at him like that for no reason? How was he to know I really had been stood up? And so what if I had! I didn't even fancy Todd. I didn't *really* fancy any guy.

The truth – and the real reason I was weeping feebly into my clenched fists – was that it didn't matter how many dates I'd been on, or could go on over the next hundred years. They were all a waste of time. Because however much I'd tried to fight it, there was absolutely no point in trying to hook up with one guy when I was still so obviously hung up on another. Josh.

Chapter 5

"I was just calling to check you hadn't forgotten about Dee's party tonight. You are still coming, aren't you?"

It was nine-thirty in the morning and Beth was on the phone. Only seconds before I'd been asleep, dreaming of Josh.

"Oh, I don't know," I yawned. "I'm not really in the mood for a party."

"But you must!" she wailed. "With four brothers in the family, there's bound to be loads of single guys there. It's the ideal place to meet someone. Anyhow, I need you to be there so we can freak out together for one last party before I go on a boring holiday with my comatose parents. Come on, girl, get a grip! You're not still moping about Todd, are you?"

I'd told Beth all about all my close shaves with the opposite sex, culminating with the non-appearance of Todd, and how I'd bumped into Josh and been really rude to him. I told her my reaction had been caused by the fact that my date hadn't bothered to turn up.

Weeks had gone by since then, and I'd hardly been out of the house. Beth had come to the conclusion that I'd OD'd on dalliances with no-hopers, which was why she was so adamant that I go with her and Josh to Dee and her hunky brothers' party. What Beth didn't realize was that I wasn't up to facing Josh, partly because I was ashamed of myself that night at the Style Café, but mostly because I was trying to avoid the surge of feelings I had for him whenever I laid eyes on him.

But Beth was determined to get me out of what she called my couch potato phase. She had me on the phone for an hour, pleading, cajoling and begging me to go, until I finally relented and said yes.

"But if I'm not having a good time, I'm coming home," I warned her as she whooped and cheered at the other end of the line. That was the trouble with Beth; she was so blooming enthusiastic about everything, it made you feel like a real killjoy if you weren't sharing her exuberance.

I came off the phone feeling like I'd been bullied into doing something I really wasn't into. God! I thought. No wonder I haven't got a boyfriend. Who'd want to go out with a misery-guts like me? I made an instant pledge to myself to buck up, cheer up, and *try* to enjoy myself.

We'd arranged to meet outside the betting shop at the end of Dee's road, and I was so grateful that Josh wasn't with Beth when I arrived. Apparently he'd gone to meet someone in town about a job he was doing the following week and would go from there straight to the party. I knew I was putting off the inevitable time when I would have to face him again, but I was still glad of the reprieve.

The party was in full swing when we arrived. People had spilled out into the front and back gardens, and window-rattling music was booming into the street and beyond. You had to holler just to be heard above the noise. It was great.

Inside, people were already copping off together and the exchange of snogging going on had reached epidemic proportions. There were couples in the kitchen, on the stairs, in the bathroom, the bedrooms – there was even one pair snogging in the airing cupboard and it wasn't even nine o'clock yet.

After grabbing a couple of beers, Beth and I

made our way straight to the centre of the party: the dance floor. A few hours ago, this was probably the living-room, but now, aside from a DJ and his mixing deck, the room had been cleared of all furniture. Even so, with forty or so people already packed in, we were hard pushed to find a space big enough to groove in.

"I don't know where Josh has got to," Beth shouted a while later. "He said he'd be here by nine."

I glanced at my watch, peering to see the time in the dimness of the room. I had to wait for a strobe light to come before I could make the Mickey Mouse face out. It felt like we'd only been here for half an hour but it was actually ten-thirty.

Beth went off to get us more drinks and look for Josh. When she came back – ages later – he was with her. I stood staring at him, transfixed. He must have sensed someone's eyes drilling into him, because he looked over in my direction, caught my eye, winked, and gave me a wave.

Phew! I thought. At least he isn't going to ignore me completely. I felt much better and, even though we hadn't actually spoken yet, it was as though the ice had been broken. I carried on dancing, then Beth came over and handed me a beer.

"He finally got here then," I said, nodding

over to where Josh was standing talking to some-one.

"Yeah, and he's drunk," Beth said, her mouth curling into a pout of disapproval. "And when I asked him where he'd been, he told me to mind my own business."

"Oh." I'd never heard Beth say anything disparaging about Josh before; they seemed like the perfect couple, all lovey-dovey and nice to – and about – each other at all times. I was a bit taken aback to say the least.

Beth was frowning; she looked a bit concerned. Then, glancing around the room, her face lit up once more.

"Ooh, look!" she cried. "There's Amanda Wakeman. I haven't seen her in ages. I must go and see whether it's true about her and Simon Fellows. Be back in a tick." And off she breezed, all fluffy happiness again. That was the best thing about Beth – she was never down in the mouth for longer than a few seconds. She's a perpetually perky person, always has been, always will be, I thought as I carried on dancing on my own. I was having a brilliant time. This was a fabulous party.

I suddenly felt a light butterfly kiss land on the nape of my neck. Surprised, I turned round to see whose lips the kiss had come from. It was

Josh. My heart rocketed into my mouth and a jolt of excitement sent an electric shock through my entire body. A split second later sense took over and started ringing alarm bells in my ears. I was his girlfriend's best friend: what the heck did he think he was doing?

"Hi, babe! Fancy dancing with me?" he smiled cheekily, then took a slurp from the bottle he was holding and swayed a little, his fragile balance upset by having to tilt his head back to swallow the mouthful of beer. Beth was right – he was out of it. Not only that, but she was only a few metres away from us, gassing to Amanda Wakeman. I was staggered.

He moved closer, near enough for me to smell the alcohol on his breath. He held both arms out in an open gesture and began grinding his body close to mine. I laughed nervously, as though I knew he was messing about, and backed off.

"What the hell do you think you're doing?" I whispered. I was embarrassed now; even in this dim light, people were noticing something was going on. Josh moved one step closer to me again and bent his head towards my face as though he was going to kiss me. I froze, terrified that Beth would see, yet excited beyond belief. Pressing his mouth close to my ear he spoke.

"You know I fancy you, don't you? I've fancied you all along." He lifted his head slightly and looked right into my eyes.

I was transfixed. My heart pounded, galloping against my insides. This couldn't be happening to me, it must be a dream. I was on a giddy rollercoaster of emotion, confused, yet exhilarated, disgusted but thrilled all at the same time. I opened my mouth to speak, though I didn't yet know what I was going to say. I tore my eyes away from him – I had to break the spell. As I looked wildly about the room, I caught sight of Beth. She was standing watching us, uncertainty etched on her face.

"Get lost!" I hissed to Josh. He moved away from me, his eyes never once leaving mine. He gave me a knowing smile and said, "I'll be back," in a passable Arnold Schwarzenegger voice. Then he lurched off, swaying unsteadily towards the kitchen and a table laden down with booze.

Next thing I knew, Beth was in my face.

"What was all that about?" she demanded, her tone suspicious.

I had to think fast, I couldn't tell her the truth.

"Blimey! You were right," I said quickly. "He's *rolling* drunk."

"What did he say to you?" she urged.

"Well, actually, he was taking the mickey out of the way I was dancing."

"You're joking! How dare he!" Beth was indignant, I suspect as much for the fact that he was drunk as for what he'd supposedly said to me. Josh being rude to me was the perfect excuse for her to have a go at him. I tried to smooth the situation over.

"Look, it's no big deal, Beth," I reasoned. "He's out of his head and doesn't know what he's saying. He didn't mean it, I'm sure, and he's probably right; I do look like a constipated chicken when I dance."

"I don't believe it! Is that what he said?" Her eyes were like saucers. Then she began to smile, and it wasn't long before we were both in fits of laughter, though for me it was more out of relief than anything else.

Before we'd had time to gather ourselves together, Dee came up and tapped Beth on the shoulder.

"Er, in case you're wondering where Josh is," she whispered, "I've just seen him throwing up in my mum's flowerbeds." She pointed in the direction of the front garden where a shapeless lump was lying in in a heap among the pansies. The sight made us laugh even more.

"Oh well, party over," Beth finally managed to

say between giggles. "I'd better get the drunken bum to a taxi and get him back to my house. Do you want a lift?"

"I think I'll pass on that one," I said. "I don't fancy having him chuck up all over me on the way home, thanks. I'll get another cab."

Nor do I want Josh doing or saying something else while I'm around, I thought. Not that he looks capable of anything at the moment.

I left the party and made my way to the mini-cab office opposite Dee's house. I had a lot to think about, not least what had happened back there. I was intrigued, nervous and dismayed. Perhaps Josh really did like me. Or was it just a drunken gesture that didn't mean anything? And why did I feel so guilty about the tingling sensation that went through my body whenever my mind replayed that kiss on my neck? Was it because my sheer longing for Josh was tantamount to disloyalty to Beth? Or because I thought – no, *hoped* – it would be a prelude to something more? I didn't have to wait long to find out.

Beth and I had arranged to go shopping a few days later, and she took great delight in telling the story of how Josh had been sick eight times after the party, then again on several occasions the morning after. Apparently he couldn't remember a thing about the party. He didn't even think he'd been there, being under the impression that he'd gone straight to Beth's after meeting his mate in town.

So the chances were, Josh didn't have a clue about what had gone on between us, I mused while staring bleakly at the window display in Miss Selfridge. I was mortified.

My mind sank into thoughts of morose self-pity. It was as though the whole evening had been some kind of cruel dream that only I knew about. Our brief encounter would be a memory that I would feed off for ever, never meeting another mouth to take the place of his, and dying a decrepit old spinster, lonely and bitter. My life was rapidly taking on tragic proportions.

As always, Beth managed to haul me back from the brink of despair with her flippant remarks and *joie de vivre*. We ended up trying on ridiculous outfits in a second-hand shop, pretending to be characters from Dickens's *Great Expectations* where I was sad old spinster Miss Haversham (ironic or what?) and she played Pip. We bought a couple of enormous straw hats, then went for tea and cream cakes where we gossiped like a couple of old washerwomen.

Beth and I never failed to have a good time

together, and it was easy to see why we were so close. I couldn't imagine life without her, which was why it was all the more hard for me to cope with the conflicting feelings going on inside my head.

We finally went our separate ways and I began walking home. I hadn't gone far when a car coming towards me began flashing its lights and tooting its horn frantically. Oh my God! I could hardly believe it. It was Josh. He pulled over to the side of the road and stuck his head out of the open window.

"Hi! I'm glad I've caught you," he said. "I was looking for you. I've just come back from your house."

I didn't even know he knew where I lived.

"You've sobered up then?" I asked. It was all I could think of to say.

"Hmm, yeah. That's why I wanted to see you." He seemed a little uneasy. "Look," he continued, "I'm really sorry about the other night."

"Oh." I was immediately put off guard. According to Beth, he didn't know anything about it.

"You mean you *do* remember?" I asked incredulously.

"Oh yes, everything. And I'm completely ashamed." .

I was crestfallen. So it was the drink talking after all.

"I handled it all wrong," he went on. "I hadn't meant to drink loads. I knew I wanted to talk to you, but I didn't have the guts to tell you sober."

"What do you mean?" What was he trying to say? Tell me *what* exactly? Talk to me about *what*?

He looked at me earnestly. "I meant what I said, you know. About fancying you."

"Wh-what?"

"Everything I said was what I feel. Do you know what I mean?"

I was stunned. "B-b-but what about Beth?"

"What about her?" he shrugged. Then he started the engine of his car again, gave me one of those infuriatingly "knowing" smiles that he'd hit me with a few times before, and drove off.

Chapter 6

I couldn't believe what was happening to me. What did Josh think he was doing, driving off like that without a proper explanation? What did he mean when he said *"What about her?"* Were they splitting up? Beth hadn't said anything – as far as she was concerned they were still an item. In fact, she'd said she was seeing Josh tonight. Maybe he was planning to break up with her then . . . but not because of me, surely? I didn't want to be the reason Josh was going to dump Beth, I couldn't be. It would destroy our friendship.

When I got home, there was an ominous message scribbled on the pad by the phone: *Ring Beth. Urgent.*

My heart was in my mouth as I dialled her

number. What if Josh had already told her? I'd never forgive myself if I was the *only* reason for the demise of their relationship. It wouldn't be so bad if he couldn't stand the way she ate, or hated the fact that she liked to talk a lot, but if it was just because he wanted to go out with me . . . I couldn't bear to think of Beth's reaction.

Her phone seemed to ring for ages before she picked it up.

"Oh, hi!" she chirruped brightly on hearing my voice. "Josh just called me. We've had a change of plan for tonight. We're not going to the cinema now, we're going to Rollerworld instead. Gavin's coming too, so do you want to make up a foursome?"

Well, I didn't expect her to say that. Josh must have called her after he'd seen me, so quite why he had the idea to go rollerblading – and palm me off with his friend – I could only wonder at. The plot thickened.

Ordinarily, I would say no way to a blind date, especially after the series of disastrous evenings I'd been out on recently. And the thought of going on a date with a guy and having your best mate pulling "Are you OK?" faces in the background all evening, while studying your every move in the minutest detail, filled me with dread.

However, it was Beth's last night before she went on holiday with her family to Wales, so it was the last time I'd see her for a week. I was intrigued to find out what Josh had planned — and what he was playing at — and, of course, it would mean seeing him again. Maybe the picture would become clearer as the evening unfolded.

So I said yes.

I spent the next four hours pampering myself and I was still hard pushed to get ready in time. I had to wash and style my hair three times before I was happy with it. I reapplied my make-up four times (at least) and changed my mind about what I was going to wear half a dozen times, even though I was only considering jeans and T-shirts. But they had to be the *right* shade of denim and the T-shirt had not only to match perfectly, but to flatter my shape as well. It was a tough job.

As I made my way to meet everyone, I was determined to blank out all possible connotations of what might happen tonight. Thinking about it only sent my mind into turmoil, so I decided to let the evening throw at me whatever surprises it chose.

Thankfully, only Beth was waiting for me outside Rollerworld.

"Come on, you're late," she chided. "They're already here, and Gavin is so gorgeous, I'm dead jealous."

I was tempted to "jokingly" offer to swap, but thought better of it. I still didn't know what Josh had up his sleeve, and whatever I said could have implications for my future friendship with Beth, so I kept my mouth shut.

She steered me towards the bar, which was empty save for a lone figure standing with his back to us.

"Gavin, this is Mel!" Beth made her announcement a little over-dramatic – I almost expected a drumroll accompaniment. He turned to me and smiled. Until now, I hadn't given a single thought to my date for the evening – he didn't come into the picture at all. So I was pleasantly surprised when I saw him. He was tall and slim, with short brown hair and an earring in one ear. He had an open, smiley face, a long pointed nose, and little creases at the corners of his eyes, which made me think he must laugh a lot. He seemed friendly enough, but he wasn't Josh. I could have been on a date with Tom Cruise and still not been interested. I only wanted Josh.

We went to hire our boots. As we stood in the queue I asked where Josh was, as casually as I could muster.

"Haven't you seen him?" said Beth. "He's already out there, showing off."

I looked over to where she was pointing. At first all I could see was a crowd of people whizzing around in a big circle. Then I picked up the figure of a lone skater among the mêlée. He was at the far end of the rink, doing tricks, complex spins and jumps, turning on a knife edge. He looked like he should be appearing in *Starlight Express* in the West End. He was awesome.

"Sickening, isn't it?" laughed Gavin. "He used to play ice hockey as a kid but he got kicked out for playing too rough. He's still brilliant though."

"You wait!" piped up Beth. "If you think he's good, you should see Mel. She's even better. Aren't you, Mel?"

"Er . . . I get by," I countered modestly and reddened slightly.

Actually, I *was* pretty good. I'd been into it for years, so this was the perfect opportunity to impress. I was a bit rusty though, not having had eight wheels on my feet for ages, and I wished I could still fit into my own boots rather than have to hire the ugly-looking cheap versions you got on site. Still, I was confident I wouldn't show myself up too much.

I swished on to the rink ahead of Beth and

Gavin and began whizzing round at great speed. After a full circuit, I caught up with them again, and giggled as I watched them gamely clinging on to each other, alarmed grins frozen to their faces. I'd only been here with Beth once before. It was her first time and within minutes she'd broken a fingernail and refused to continue. She obviously wasn't faring much better now. Gavin could go forward at a snail's pace, but that was about it. As a pair, they were useless.

I put myself between them to steady them and we set off round the rink in a sedate fashion. As we passed Josh, Beth called out to him for help. He turned and burst out laughing at the sight of us. Beth and Gavin's outside arms were swirling round like windmills, while my body acted like a rock of support in the middle. He breezed over and – without even acknowledging I was there – took Beth by both hands and led her off, him travelling backwards while she flapped about like an irate budgie. Within seconds, she was in a heap on the floor, her limbs splayed like a starfish. Struggling to rise, she looked like a newborn deer trying to get up for the first time – even with Josh's help it took three attempts.

"Right, that's it," she wailed. "I've had

enough. I'm going for a coffee. If God had meant us to wheel ourselves around the world, he would have given us castors instead of feet." Grabbing at a side wall, she headed for a gap and flounced off.

Meanwhile, Gavin was heading gingerly in the same direction. "Wait for me!" he yelled. "I could do with a rest too." He slithered off.

"And what about you, Mel? Do you need a hand getting around?" Josh looked at me, that irritatingly knowing smile plastered all over his face.

"I think I can manage," I said, adding a smug "Catch me if you can!" as I set off round the rink as fast as I could. My getaway rendered him stationary for a few seconds, so I turned to wave at him and saw him standing there, his mouth open in surprise. Then he set off in pursuit, and we ended up roaring around in a game of cat and mouse. We were racing much faster than anyone else, weaving in and out of the crowd, matching each other for speed and agility. I was laughing hysterically, determined to keep one step ahead of him, but at the same time knowing I'd let him catch me eventually.

Then I put in a dirty stop, and, turning on the spot, watched as he sailed past me, unable to halt as abruptly or as smoothly as I had. As I expected, this was like a red rag to a bull. When he did finally turn, he sped towards me, a huge grin on his face. But instead of speeding by as I thought, he skidded to a halt. Misjudging how quickly he could stop, however, he cannoned into me and we both went crashing to the floor.

Our bodies entwined as we fell and my breath was completely knocked out of me. It wasn't caused by the fall, but by the sheer thrill of coming into contact with Josh's chest, arms, thighs. . . He had a firm hold of me round the waist, and he wasn't letting go. We lay there for what seemed like for ever, me with my head on his chest, feeling his hot breath on my face. He began stroking my back with his fingers, slowly and methodically. It was so erotic, it was almost unbearable. I could stay like this for ever, I thought, but I was terrified Beth would be watching. I pulled away and leapt up. It was a good job I did, because the next moment I heard Beth's voice loud and clear and very near.

"Hey, you two! Over here!" she called from the other side of the barrier about two metres away. "Gav and I are starving so we're going for a burger instead," she explained. "Are you coming, or are you both going to carry on trying to break the land speed record?"

"Mmm, I'm starving," Josh said from the floor. "Give us a hand up, Mel."

I held out my hand and he took it and hauled himself upright. He gave it a little squeeze before letting go and I melted into a damp puddle on the floor.

"I was watching you out there," said Gavin. "Beth was right – you really are good." I was back on terra firma now and Gavin came and stood beside me and went to put his arm around my shoulder. I cringed inside and moved away, bending down to take off my boots. I hoped I'd made it obvious that I didn't want him anywhere near me and deliberately walked ahead of everyone on our way to the burger bar.

I felt acutely uncomfortable throughout our meal. On one side of me was Gavin, desperately trying to engage me in a conversation consisting of more than one-word answers. On the other I had Josh's eyes digging into me so that I daren't look up from my plate for fear of the mesmerizing effect they had on me. And sitting opposite was Beth, who jabbered away, totally oblivious to the situation. I didn't eat a thing and desperately wished I could be somewhere else, preferably with Josh.

When I excused myself to escape to the loo,

Beth came rushing in after me. She'd taken my silence and lack of appetite completely the wrong way.

"You fancy Gav, don't you?" she cajoled me. "I can tell. You've hardly said a word all evening and you pushed your fries around your plate like they were going to poison you. Shall I suggest we all go out again when I get back from my hols?"

Oh no! I couldn't bear another evening like this.

"Um, no," I said, panic written across my face. I tried desperately to think of a good excuse to get out of here *and* get out of another date with Gavin.

"He seems nice, but he's not my type," I ventured. "The truth is, I'm not feeling too well — bit of a stomach upset. It wasn't too bad earlier on, but the sight of all that food began making me feel sick. I might head for home if you don't mind."

"You poor thing!" consoled Beth, real concern written on her face. "I had no idea. We'll go now, shall we?"

I nodded gratefully, glad of the chance to escape further scrutiny.

I felt like a fraud going back to the table. Beth had already hurried on ahead, no doubt to announce my impending death. Gavin looked anxious for me and took my hand and patted it when I sat down (euch!), while Josh just winked and smiled when no one was looking.

As we got up and headed for the exit, Josh peeled off from the group and disappeared around the corner, saying he was going to the loo. He was gone for a good ten minutes and when he finally came sauntering back to us, he had a big smirk on his face.

Beth eyed him suspiciously. "You've been gone for ages. Where have you been?"

"Mind your own business," he snarled, the smirk disappearing to be replaced by a hard look in his eyes.

"You could have said. We would have gone to the bar if we'd known we were going to have to wait so long for you to show your face—"

"What *is* this?" snarled Josh. "The third degree? I bumped into a mate, not that it's got anything to do with you. Now, can we please go?"

We trooped out silently. I couldn't believe Beth's outburst. What was her problem? Today had been a real eye-opener for me. It was the first time I'd seen cracks in their relationship. Maybe Beth knew things weren't right between her and Josh. Maybe she sensed he was going to finish it.

When we got to Josh's car, he offered to drop us off at Beth's. Although I would have preferred not to spend another fifteen minutes in an enclosed space with Gavin's unwanted attention, I felt it churlish to refuse.

I wedged myself into the corner of the back seat, but it didn't stop Gavin from sitting far too close and trying to talk to me all the way home. I gave vague answers to his questions and spent most of the journey avoiding eye contact by staring out of the window. Inside I was fuming.

God! Why is it that blokes are so thick sometimes? They never take the hint, they've got no idea about body language, and they can't ever imagine a girl wouldn't fancy them. And if I wasn't such a wimp I would have put him straight by now, I thought, which infuriated me even more.

A loud voice woke me from my pensive thoughts.

"Mel! *Hello, Mel!* Earth to Mel!"

I looked up to see Beth watching me from the front seat and laughing.

"Wh-what? Sorry, I was miles away."

"I said, do you want to come out again as soon as I get back from Wales?"

"Um, yeah, sure. I'd love to." *Not likely. Not if*

Gavin's coming too, I thought bitterly.

We'd arrived at Beth's house and I leapt out of the car practically before Josh had pulled into the side of the road.

"I'll walk you home," Gavin said hopefully.

"No, really, don't worry. I don't live far away."

But the ignoramus wasn't taking no for an answer. "You're on my way home. I insist," he said in an irritatingly sincere voice.

I relented, said good-night to Beth and Josh who were still sitting in the car, and stomped off at 100 miles an hour. I was convinced Josh was smirking at me, revelling in my discomfort, as I disappeared down the road. For the life of me, I couldn't work him out.

Then it dawned on me. Gavin was the perfect opportunity to try and find out some more about Josh. After all, if his friend didn't know him, who did? I slowed a bit, allowing him to catch me up.

"So, how long have you and Josh known each other?" I asked.

"Years," he replied. "We used to be at school together. Josh left at sixteen though, while I carried on to do A Levels."

So you had the brains, while he got the looks, I thought, wishing I was walking home with Josh rather than his friend. Gavin took my sudden inquisitiveness to mean that I was interested in *him*, and spent the next few minutes telling me how well he'd done at school and how deeply fascinating his engineering course was at university.

I didn't listen to a word, instead fantasizing about Josh and what we'd talk about if he was here. Actually, we probably wouldn't be doing that much talking at all. Instead, we'd be investigating the finer points of tonsil hockey. The very thought made me go weak at the knees.

Coming back to the real world and realizing that Gavin was still droning on, I decided to bring the conversation back to a much more interesting subject.

"So," I cut in, "does Josh have any hidden talents, other than rollerblading, that we should know about?" I knew I sounded just like that wally Danny, dating me then asking all about Beth, but I couldn't help myself, and just hoped Gavin wouldn't cotton on that I fancied his mate.

"Not as far as I know," he said. "I think he keeps himself to himself as much as possible. He's usually up to no good in some way or another."

I was intrigued. "What do you mean, *up to no good*?"

"Look, Mel," Gavin said gently, "there's a lot

you and Beth don't know about Josh, and you're best off out of it."

"What *do* you mean?" I repeated, my eyes agog. "Best off out of what?"

"Just be careful, OK."

We walked on in silence. I didn't want to believe what I was hearing, I wanted to dismiss it as hyperbole, but something made me think Gavin was telling the truth. Josh had never struck me as anything other than charming, smart and a thoroughly pleasant person, not someone who you needed to be warned away from. Maybe I ought to say something to Beth. . .

We were at my house now. I thanked Gavin for walking me home, and started up the path to the front door.

"Hold on," he called, coming after me. "Can I ring you sometime?" He immediately looked taken aback by his forthrightness and coloured from the neck upwards. "I . . . um . . . mean," he spluttered nervously, "only if you don't mind."

I smiled weakly and thought fast. "Um, why don't you give me your phone number? I'll ring you when I'm feeling better."

I dragged an old bus ticket out of my bag and handed it over to him. He looked pleased as he scribbled the number down and pressed the ticket back into my hand. I muffled a goodbye and shoved my key into the lock. Grinding the piece of paper angrily into the palm of my hand, I opened the door, went inside, walked to the kitchen and threw his number in the bin.

Chapter 7

I felt I owed it to Beth to put her in the picture about what Gavin had said about Josh – assuming she didn't already know. So I rang her early next morning, hoping to catch her before she went away.

"Hi!" she trilled. "How are you feeling? I hope you didn't spew all over Gavin, hee hee!"

"Nearly," I said, then, feigning uppitiness, added, "particularly when he asked me for my phone number."

"How very forward of him!" She shrieked, laughing. "You know, he's such a nice guy, I was hoping he'd grow on you, even though you said last night that he wasn't your type. That was why I suggested another evening out, but I guess you're not up for it."

"I don't think so," I said scathingly. "I know this sounds weird, but he's a bit *too* nice, if you know what I mean. We had quite an enlightening chat about Josh on the way home, though."

"And?" She sounded curious.

"Well, Gavin seemed to think he was up to no good."

"What do you mean – like in trouble with the police?"

"I don't know," I said, then relayed the conversation I'd had with Gavin. Beth didn't sound surprised.

"I know he's been in trouble when he was younger because he says he was always getting thrown out of school, but he also said that was all behind him. . ." She stopped short and I heard a noise in the background. Someone was calling to her.

"I'm going to have to go – that's Dad shouting," she said. "The car's loaded up and they're waiting for me. I'll try and call you sometime in the week."

I quickly wished her a good time and came off the phone feeling none the wiser. There was obviously a lot more to Josh than I'd first thought, and I was intrigued to know more.

I didn't have to wait long to find out.

* * *

By the time Beth had been away for two days, I was bored stiff and wishing she was back. I really missed her company when she wasn't around. Of course I had other mates – it's not like I'm a Mrs No Friends, or anything – but there was no one I felt like I could drone on to about nothing in particular for hours on end.

To try and dig myself out from a rut of boredom I decided to go window-shopping in town. I was breezing through the mall towards Miss Selfridge and fantasizing about the acres of clothes I'd buy if I won the Lottery when I saw Josh heading in my direction. I could hardly believe my eyes as I stared, but it was definitely him. My pulse went into overdrive and my mouth suddenly did an impression of the Sahara desert. I wondered if he would spot me as he got nearer, but he looked like he was a million miles away, staring into the distance, a blank expression on his face.

Just as he was a metre or so away from me he seemed to click back to reality and look around him. Then he saw me and smiled and came right over.

"Fancy seeing you here," he grinned, while I attempted to gather myself back together after the devastating effect the mere sight of him had had on me. "What are you up to?" he continued.

"Er . . . nothing in particular. Just window-shopping really. . ." My voice tailed off as I couldn't think of anything else to say. His appearance had taken me so completely by surprise.

"If you're not in a hurry to get anywhere, do you fancy going for a coffee?" he asked, adding, "I'm gasping."

I nodded eagerly (too eagerly?) and we walked to one of those café places that you find in the middle of shopping malls, where you sit and watch fraught people stumbling about, struggling with their shopping bags and baby buggies and kids. As we made our way there I tried vainly to think of some riveting topics to keep him entertained but couldn't, my brain having turned to mashed potato.

Fortunately Josh never seemed to be short of anything to say and he kept the conversation going, however one-sided it was. Quite why he had any desire to spend time with a mute munchkin like me I could only wonder at.

"I was looking for some new gear, but all the shops round here are really naff," he chattered as we walked. "I think I'm going to end up going to London for a day. You know, splash out a bit."

By now we were at the counter which served

coffee, croissants and baguettes. Josh ordered a coffee for him and a cappuccino for me and we waited as the waitress revved up the cappuccino maker and I searched the corners of my brain for something interesting to say in reply. After what seemed like an age, something popped into my head and I spoke.

"If you wait until Beth gets back I'm sure she'd love to go to London with you," I announced, looking at him, then wondered what I'd said wrong as the whole character of his face changed. His look went from being jovial to utterly despondent in the space of about two seconds. He looked down at the floor and began fiddling nervously with the teaspoon at the side of the cup he was carrying towards an empty table in a corner of the seating area. Then he cleared his throat as though he was about to say something important.

"She hasn't told you then," he answered mysteriously.

"Told me what?" I asked, frowning.

"We . . . it's a bit hard to say. . . You see, we had a huge row before she went away. . ." He broke off for a few seconds, and then continued, ". . .and well, we ended up splitting up."

"Oh!" I exclaimed, stunned. "I had no idea. She didn't say anything to me, and I spoke to her just as she was about to leave."

"Well, it only happened literally as the family was about to drive away for their holiday," he went on. "We'd had a bit of a barney the night before, so I went round on Saturday to patch things up. But I just made matters worse."

"Oh." What else could I say? I was completely taken aback by what I was hearing. I was surprised that Beth hadn't mentioned something to me about a row with Josh. She was never one to suppress her emotions. But then, we *had* only spoken for a few seconds on Saturday, before her dad made her get off the phone. Perhaps when she said she'd call me, it was to tell me about the latest developments with Josh.

I was unsure of what to say. I didn't want to appear too nosy by asking what had happened; after all, it wasn't really any of my business. On the other hand, it did seem like he wanted to tell me, otherwise he would never have brought the subject of an argument up. Josh solved my dilemma for me. Taking a couple of slurps from his coffee cup, he put it back on its saucer and spoke.

"You might have already noticed that things haven't been going too well for us recently," he said, a weary tone in his voice. "It culminated in the fight we had at the end of the night when we all went rollerblading together, after you and Gavin had gone home. I felt that Beth was becoming a bit of a nag, wanting to know where I was and who I was with every second of the day, not letting me have a life of my own. I was starting to feel trapped and I told her so. She got on the defensive and ended up storming off into her house.

"So I went round the following day to try and put things right. But I picked totally the wrong moment where she was in a hurry and her dad was hassling her to get in the car. She just blew up at me again and dumped me."

He gave me a resigned look and shrugged.

"So that's it," he added, draining the coffee from his cup. "Finished. The end."

"But surely you can patch things up?" I cried, aghast. "I'm sure Beth doesn't want it to end like this. She really liked you."

He shrugged again. "And I really liked her too. But you know, the hard truth is that I don't *want* to patch things up. I know this may sound heartless, but I really think our relationship wasn't going anywhere, and I think Beth knew it too, even if she never said anything to you. Or even admitted it to herself. Maybe it's for the best that it happened like this. It was getting a bit intense between us. It's probably a good thing that we're having this break from each other. It'll add to the finality of the situation."

"It sounds like you've already made your mind up," I said.

"I have," he replied. "Look, don't get me wrong. I think Beth is a great girl, brilliant fun and totally gorgeous. But I don't think she's the one for me." He broke off and began shifting uneasily in his seat. He was fiddling with the sugar bowl now, smoothing the pile of little crystals into a flat surface with the back of a tea-spoon, then drawing wavy lines across the sugar with the edge of the spoon.

"What do you mean?" I asked, my eyes fixed on the patterns he was creating.

He looked up, which made me do the same and we looked at each other. He gave me a little smile and I felt my cheeks colour and my mouth go dry again.

"I just don't think Beth and I had any future together," he replied, looking deep into my eyes.

What about us, Josh? I thought. *Have we got a future together?*

"I think it's much better that we finish it now before one of us gets in too deep and gets hurt," he continued. "I'm sure it won't be long before Beth gets another boyfriend, one much better suited to her than me. And, well, I feel pretty awful now, but I guess I'll pick myself up and bounce back soon enough."

He reached out his hand and touched mine, giving it a little squeeze from across the table and shooting a spasm of excitement through my body. For a moment I thought he was going to leave it there, but he didn't, instead drawing it back before carrying on speaking.

"Anyway, thanks for listening to me ramble on," he said. "I'm glad I've put you in the picture. I feel much better now I've got it all off my chest. I was actually pretty down about it all until I bumped into you. I've even been turning down party invitations because I can't be bothered to go to them."

"Oh no, you must go out and try and have a good time!" I exclaimed. "There's nothing worse than sitting around feeling sorry for yourself – you'll only get even more depressed. I know, because it's the sort of thing I'd do. You need to get out and take your mind off what's happened."

"Maybe you're right," he said with a half-smile. Then, visibly brightening, he almost leapt out of his seat as though he'd suddenly hit on a great idea. He became much more animated as he spoke.

"Listen," he said. "I've been invited to a party tomorrow night with a load of friends. I didn't much feel like going before today. But you know, I think you're absolutely right. I will make the effort and go, and you're welcome to come along too. How about it?"

"Gr-great. I'd love to," I stuttered nervously, desperately hoping I didn't sound too keen.

"I can meet you somewhere," he continued. "The Style Café if you like. It *was* the place we first met, after all."

He grinned mischievously and my mind whirled around in confusion. What was happening here? Was Josh asking me out? If that was the case then he'd certainly got over the grief of splitting up with Beth pretty quickly. Maybe he was just asking me to go as a friend? If so, then what was all that stuff the other day about, when he said he fancied me? I couldn't work any of it out.

"Er . . . sure," I replied, vaguely. "Whatever."

"You'll know a few people there, I'm sure," he went on. "Gavin's going. . ."

So that was it! He was trying to set me up with Gavin again. The rat!

"But don't let that stop you from coming," he continued. "I got the feeling you two didn't get it together the other night. Don't worry, though –

I'll protect you from him." He laughed out loud and slapped his hand on the table in front of him like he'd just made a really funny joke.

"I must go," he said, looking at his watch and leaping from his seat. "So, I'll meet you at seven-thirty, OK? Bring a bottle and – look, er . . . thanks for today. See you tomorrow."

And with that he was gone, rushing off into the distance, a totally different figure from the one I'd bumped into a short time ago.

I sat in my seat for an age, doodling with the sugar bowl and pondering what had just happened. I really couldn't make much sense of what was going on. I certainly didn't feel totally comfortable with what was happening. I felt like I needed to speak to Beth, to hear her side of the story.

I was sure Josh was interested in me, and yes, I was desperate to go out with him, but only if he and Beth had definitely broken up and she was happy about the situation.

But then, maybe I was reading too much into all this. Josh might have invited hundreds of girls to this party, just as he might tell different girls he fancied them ten times a day. He might be that sort of person.

I finally came to the conclusion that the best thing for me to do was take a rain check on my emotions and just go along to this party to have fun. Anything else that might happen would then be a bonus.

Chapter 8

It felt like I'd been waiting for this party all my life. It felt like I'd known Josh even longer. And now I was sick with nerves. However much I tried to convince myself that this was just another party, and that I was going with Josh *as a friend*, I couldn't suppress the expectation and tension that kept fizzing about in my stomach. I had to keep telling myself that nothing was going to happen between us.

I tried to imagine that I was going on a date with Brad Pitt, and that was why I was feeling so nervous. I decided I was making the extra effort over clothes and how I would look because Brad was more used to dating sophisticated Hollywood stars, not girls from nondescript towns in England.

Actually, it didn't matter if I was dressing to impress Brad or Josh – I was still acutely aware that the contents of my wardrobe were a disaster. After Josh had left me in the café at the mall, I spent the rest of the day leaping in and out of changing rooms, huffing and puffing my way into clothes, becoming increasingly frantic in my quest to find something stunning to wear.

Normally, I relished the opportunity to shop and actually buy something. But not now. My search proved fruitless and I ended up going home empty handed and in the depths of despair. I realized I would have to rely on an existing outfit, maybe something I knew I looked OK in. In fact, I convinced myself, that was probably a better idea anyway. Much more sensible to wear an old favourite than new gear that I might decide I looked gross in after a couple of hours' wear.

However, even the stuff that I'd worn time after time with great success seemed dreadful now. Clothes which would have been perfectly adequate twenty-four hours earlier became fit only for the local rummage sale. Tops that I'd worn a hundred times with no qualms whatsoever suddenly made me look too fat, top heavy or flat-chested (delete as applicable), and clothes I'd bought just weeks before were now frumpy or trashy. Nothing was good enough.

By the following morning I was desperate. I'd been up since seven and had narrowed an abysmal choice down to two dresses, one green, one orange, both hideous (or so I thought in the warped state of mind I was in). One of them would have to do.

I chose the green because it made my hips look a millimetre smaller than the orange and started planning my accessories and make-up around it. This took another two hours of deliberation before I realized that if I didn't get in the bath – like NOW – I wouldn't be ready in time.

A couple of litres of Body Shop bubble bath went sloshing into the running water. I held my face over the steaming bath for a few minutes then peered into the magnified side of a mirror and began attacking a glut of blackheads on my nose. And chin. And forehead. By the time I'd finished I swear my face looked worse than before I'd started.

I lay in the bath until my skin had shrunk and my hands looked like shrivelled-up cocktail sausages. It was three-thirty by the time I emerged from the bathroom slathered in lotions and potions, oils and perfume, an aroma of high flammability wafting towards my bedroom.

The next few hours whizzed by as I tweaked

and teased my hair into a voluminous creation of curls around my head. The usually rebellious twists of hair allowed me to take control for once, and gave me more time to concentrate on my make-up, which I left understated apart from a slash of cherry red lipstick across my mouth.

I gathered my chosen outfit together, slowly got dressed and studied my reflection in the full-length mirror on my bedroom door. I looked . . . OK. In fact, I was quite pleasantly surprised. I'd expected to look like something out of a low budget horror movie, so the almost girlish-looking person staring back at me was a bit of a shock. It felt like a good omen for the evening ahead.

The phone rang. It was six-forty-five and I was ready with ten minutes to spare before I had to leave. I'd been so organized I even had time to answer it. I picked up the receiver and said hello.

"Hello, Mel, it's me."

Josh! Why was he calling so late in the day? My whole world stopped and held its breath.

"I'm really glad I caught you," he said. "Look, something's come up. I can't meet you."

My heart disappeared into my boots. I couldn't believe it! He wasn't coming. I felt like weeping. I vaguely heard his voice through the fuzz of misery that had begun to wash over me.

"I've got to wait around at home for a mate to drop off some money he owes me. You don't fancy coming here, do you? It's on the way to the party, so we can go on from here."

It's OK! He's not bailing out after all. My heart soared again and exploded out of the top of my head. He gave me directions to where he lived, and as I came off the phone I kissed it with happiness.

I ordered a taxi because I didn't want to risk ruining the day's efforts by having to run for a bus, and paced up and down my room while I waited for it to turn up. When it did I passed on Josh's instructions to the driver and sat in the back of the cab, my hands clasped together, my stomach becoming increasingly bilious the nearer we got to his house. By the time we turned into his road, I wished I'd had a glass of wine before I left to calm myself. The only reason I didn't was because I thought he'd smell it and think I was a lush. Or worse, a nervous lush.

I paid the driver, walked up the path to the front door, took a deep breath and pressed the buzzer. I'd run a hundred and one opening gambits through my mind in the past day but at the vital moment they'd all deserted me. As Josh opened the door I had to settle for a plain "Hi".

He looked breathtaking standing there in a crisp white collarless shirt and jeans, his hair still wet and tousled from the shower. As always he seemed completely at ease with himself as he grinned and stepped aside, waiting for me to go in. I felt like a silly schoolgirl in comparison.

"He's not here yet," he said. "Shall we have a drink while we wait?"

I nodded, my brain taking a few seconds to work out that he was talking about the friend who owed him money. He led me into the sitting-room. It wasn't how I imagined at all – it was surprisingly neat and tidy and there were few masculine touches: I'd expected there to be a few guy-like things, maybe two-metre-tall speakers and an enormous sound system dominating the room. But no, the decor wasn't that much different from a lot of people's houses, with flowery wallpaper and chintzy curtains. There was a grotesque standard lamp in the corner and various bits of 1970s-style wooden furniture scattered about the place.

"I know what you're thinking," he said. "You're wondering what the hell I'm doing living on the set of *Coronation Street*, aren't you?"

I burst out laughing. He was absolutely right, it was like someone's sitting-room in *Corrie* or *EastEnders*.

"It's my mum – she's very traditional in her choice of decoration. She hasn't come into the Nineties yet. Thankfully, I don't share her taste. My bedroom's not nearly so naff."

My face went scarlet at the mention of his bedroom, but thankfully, if he noticed, he didn't comment on it, instead steering me towards the enormous brown and orange flowery sofa that seemed to take up the entire room.

"Disgusting, isn't it?" he said nodding his head towards it. "Do you want gin or wine?"

"Wine, please," I said, still clutching the bottle of Mateus Rosé I'd brought with me. "Do you want to make a start on this or keep it for the party?"

"We'll keep it for later," he said as he headed for the kitchen.

I began to calm down. He brought in an enormous glass of wine and a gin and tonic for himself and I settled into the sofa. I was quite surprised when he plonked himself down at the other end and sprawled out so that his knees were almost on my thighs and his feet were dangling dangerously close to my calves. I was acutely aware that we were so close and hardly dared move for fear of accidentally brushing against him. I took a gulp of wine.

"So," I said, "tell me about this party. Will I know anyone there?"

He reeled off names that meant nothing to me, then told me funny little stories about each person that made me laugh so much I felt I knew them as well as he did.

About an hour after I'd arrived, Josh phoned his friend to try and discover the reason for his non-appearance, but could get no reply, so we drank some more wine and the conversation flowed more easily and I realized I was having a wonderful time and would quite happily sit here all night talking and not go out at all. Which was really spooky, because about a second after this thought went through my head, he came out with almost the same thing.

"I don't know about you," he said, "but I really don't feel like going out now. We could just stay here and talk and get to know each other a bit better. What do you think?"

He moved closer to me on the sofa. Then he leaned forward and I sensed that he was about to kiss me. I closed my eyes and suddenly a terrible voice boomed through my head. What about Beth? it hollered. *What about Beth?*

My eyes snapped open and I shied away from him.

"What about Beth?" I was saying it out loud now, a tone of urgency in my voice.

"What?" Josh looked astonished.

"Look," I said. "I know you said you'd split up, but it feels like I'm jumping into her shoes before they're off her feet. I just don't feel very comfortable with this."

"What on earth do you mean?" He looked totally flummoxed by my outburst.

"I mean, it's not even as though I've been able to speak to her about it," I continued, thinking aloud, almost.

"So if that's the case, what are you doing here, sitting on my sofa drinking wine with me?" he asked, a twinkle in his eye and a slightly wonky smile on his face.

"I, erm . . . I'm not sure," I replied, realizing how pathetic and nonsensical I was sounding.

Josh sighed. "Listen to me," he said. "Beth and I are no longer an item. So who I go out with no longer has anything to do with her."

"But she's my best friend, and I feel like I owe it to her to at least make sure she's cool about me and you."

He took hold of my hand and looked at me earnestly. "Haven't you worked it out yet?" he quizzed. "The whole reason I finished with her was because of you. I want to be with you, Mel. Like I said the other day, it's you I fancy, not Beth, or anyone else for that matter."

I lifted my head and looked into his eyes. I'd

never been close enough to study them before but they were a beautifully rich shade of brown, like chocolate, so dark you were hard pushed to pick out the black pupils in the middle.

His eyes locked on mine and we stayed like that for what seemed like ages, neither daring to speak or breathe. Then he took his gaze away from mine and his eyes travelled down my face to my lips. I felt mine do the same, my gaze coming to rest at his mouth. His lips parted slightly and he moved towards me and they came to rest lightly on my mouth.

Then he kissed me.

The effect was sensational. I'd kissed boys before and felt nothing, and I'd come to the conclusion that all kisses were the same – they were just something you did with a boy to pass the time. But this was different, it was mind-blowing. My insides exploded and my legs started to quiver. I felt a tingling sensation throughout my body. It was heaven. His tongue began to explore the inside of my mouth, probing and prodding, stroking my tongue with his, gently biting my lips with his teeth. Again, the effect was totally different from anything ever before, delicious and erotic rather than something that made me want to clean my teeth as soon as it was over.

Then he pulled away and sat looking at me, the corners of his eyes wrinkling as he smiled.

"Come on," he finally said, "let's go upstairs."

I nodded and, still holding my hand, he pulled me gently from my seat and we stood up together, holding hands.

"Are you sure about this?" he asked, concerned.

I nodded again, too tense with excitement to speak.

"Won't your parents be worrying where their little girl has got to?" he said, a slightly mocking tone in his voice.

"They're away for a long weekend so they won't miss me at all," I managed to answer breathily.

"So I could have come round to your house then, and we wouldn't have been disturbed."

"Yes, but then we'd have had longer to travel to the party."

"What party is that then?" he said, gently stroking my arm with his hand.

I looked quizzically at him. "So you mean, there wasn't one?"

"I'm not saying that," he replied impishly, "just that as soon as I saw you walk through the door, I knew we wouldn't be going anywhere."

He bent his head and kissed me again, a kiss

which had the same devastating effect on me, only this time it made my knees almost buckle from under me too. It was a good job he had his arms around me or I was sure I would have collapsed into a heap on the carpet.

After what seemed like blissful eternity we broke apart and he led me up the stairs and into his bedroom. He closed the door behind us and turned to face me.

I didn't dare to imagine what would happen next. The anticipation was unbearable. But in the back of my mind I knew exactly what I was doing and I felt fully in control of the situation, if not my emotions. I slid my hands under his shirt and up the curve of his back to his shoulders. His skin was warm and smooth, his smell totally delicious. I pulled him towards me and pressed his body into mine. I lifted my head and watched as he bent to plant tiny, light kisses on my face, nose, neck, shoulder. We moved towards the bed while we kissed. Then, as we got to the edge of the bed I reached up, undid the top button of his shirt, and began to undress him.

He moved his hands around my back and felt for the zip of my dress, sliding it expertly down then running his hands over my bare back. He then slipped the shoulder straps away from my body and lowered his head to kiss my naked shoulders. Butterfly kisses rained down on me, smothering me in warmth and need and lust. Making me feel wanted.

We undressed each other slowly, sexily, taking it in turns to remove an item of clothing. Once naked, we lay down on the bed and wrapped our bodies around each other, all the time kissing and touching and stroking. We weren't in any hurry. I knew we had all night, and anyway, I was enjoying this. Never had I felt so relaxed and at ease with myself in such a situation. I knew my inhibitions had been loosened a little by the two glasses of wine I'd drunk, but it was more than that. I felt confident about myself and my body and what I was doing. More than ever before, I felt needed and loved and desired. What more could anyone ask for?

Chapter 9

"Uuuurrooof!"

The noise jolted me out of a deep sleep and back into the real world. I opened my eyes and a blinding white light shot a stabbing pain through my head, making me flip them shut again. Only the torture didn't subside, it got worse. My brain thumped against the sides of my skull like an enormous pulse beating furiously, trying to escape. My tongue felt like a pile of rubble, my mouth the Gobi desert. I tried opening my eyes again, this time much more carefully, so they were just a couple of slits viewing the world before me.

I looked around me, ever so slowly so as not to set off the time bomb inside my head. I recognized nothing. I was lying in an unfamiliar bed in a strange room. I was alone. The alien sound that woke me up must have been me, or at least my brain, crying out for some attention.

I was disorientated for a few moments. Where was I? What had happened? It was daytime – that much I knew: sunlight was streaming in through a chink in the curtains drawn at the window. I was lying in a double bed, and, as I squinted at the scene in front of me, I saw clothes strewn around the room. My clothes, along with someone else's. Slowly, the events of the previous night began to unravel in my head. The wine, the conversation, the kissing, the sex, Josh – it all came flooding back in a befuddled jumble.

"Ooooourgh!" I groaned again. Oh no! What had I done? I hadn't *meant* to sleep with him – the thought hadn't even entered my head before I stepped over the threshold into his house. It wasn't planned, it just happened. Why didn't I eat anything before I went out to soak up the wine I'd drunk? Probably because I was so nervous I couldn't face the thought of food. It was no wonder I had a headache.

Little snatches of last night's action played inside my head. It was as though it had been a dream, and not a particularly fabulous one at that. What I could remember – which wasn't much – wasn't anything to write home about.

After the sensuous and erotic kissing earlier on in the evening, the actual sex itself was a bit of an anticlimax. I was only grateful we had used a condom.

I needed water. I struggled up into a sitting position. The clanging in my head moved up a couple of gears in protest. I quickly lay down again. Where was Josh? I wondered. In the bathroom? Where was the bathroom? Wherever he was, I hoped he would stay there. I didn't want him to see me like this. If I looked anything like I did every other morning, I'd be a total mess. I'd have a bird's nest instead of hair and Marks and Spencer's luggage department under my eyes. A few new spots would have moved in for good measure, and I'd have breath like a rancid cabbage. Not pleasant.

I sat up again. The clattering continued but this time I ignored it. I had to get a drink and sort my face out, Josh or no Josh. I grabbed the crumpled white shirt he'd been wearing last night, slipped it on, and stood up. The room spun round and I felt exceedingly unsteady on my feet. I walked my way round the bedroom furniture like a baby taking its first wobbly steps, and tried to make my way to the door without falling over.

It was strange, but I couldn't hear a sound

from anywhere in the house. If Josh was here, he was being very quiet.

I stumbled from the room and on to the first floor landing. I had a choice of two other doors in front of me, which flummoxed my last dying brain cell for a few moments. In this sort of state, choosing between the two was like trying to pass a Mensa test. I finally plumped for the one on the left, opened the door and walked into another bedroom.

The room looked like it had been occupied very recently; it had a lived-in smell about it, the double bed wasn't made, and the wardrobe doors were ajar, revealing a glimpse of someone's clothes. I guessed rather obviously that it was his mum's room. Unable to take anything else in, with no way of making any more sense of it, my thoughts once more turned to the insatiable quest for water.

I closed the door and opened the other one. I was relieved to find that it was indeed the bathroom. Shutting the door behind me, I locked myself in and stood in front of the sink, holding on to its cool white porcelain sides for support.

I looked in the mirror in front of me and groaned at the gargoyle staring back. I looked even worse than I had imagined. I bet Josh took one look at me in bed next to him this morning and fled the house in fright.

I guzzled two glasses of water and washed my face. I felt a fraction better but not much. I was in a dilemma. Do I stay in this bathroom for the rest of my life, or do I venture downstairs and face him, even though it would mean him seeing me looking like a pig? Much as I would have happily stayed put, I realized it wasn't practical. I opened the door and crept downstairs.

Still no noise. And no sign of Josh. I ventured into the kitchen. On the table was a note:

Gone to work. Help yourself to coffee. Josh. x

The relief was mixed with a tinge of disappointment. What, no breakfast in bed? No goodbye kiss? No *"See you later, darling."* No *"What are you doing this evening?"* Just a *"Help yourself to coffee"*. Get real, girl! I scolded. Pull yourself together. Contrary to popular belief, life isn't a Mills and Boon romance.

I padded back upstairs, got dressed at great speed, and left the house.

As I made my way home the one huge problem to come out of the last few hours dominated my thoughts: Beth. Guilt weighed heavily on my shoulders. OK, so Josh was adamant that it was all over between them, but that shouldn't have given me the green light to jump into bed with him as soon as she was out of the picture. So what the hell was I thinking of when I did? The only conclusion I could come to was that I wasn't thinking at all.

I contemplated the effect my action would have on Beth. Assuming that they *had* split up, and that Beth had gone skipping off to Wales, delighted to be rid of him once and for all, then I was prepared to take bets that she'd still be severely hacked off that her best friend had done the dirty on her only days later. I knew I would be. She'd feel hurt, betrayed, angry. Why the heck hadn't I thought of all this *before* last night? Probably because I genuinely hadn't intended going all the way with Josh – it had just happened.

Not that that would be anything other than a lame excuse for Beth. She would hate me for this, and it was slowly dawning on me that, unless I was very much mistaken, it would undoubtedly destroy my relationship with her. I tried to fathom out whether a night of passion with Josh – no, let me stick my neck out here and imagine it turned out to be a proper relationship – was worth sacrificing my life-long friendship with Beth for. Whichever way I looked at it, the only conclusion I kept coming to was that Beth was worth a damn sight more to me than Josh. Even if he turned out to be the love of my life, it still couldn't compare to the friendship I had with Beth. I knew I had to do something to try and salvage the situation, but I didn't have a clue as to what. Little did I realize as I pondered my fate that events were about to take a turn for the worse.

By the following day I still hadn't heard from Josh. If I'd had the balls, I'd have been round to his house by now demanding an audience with him. If I'd had half a brain I would have located his phone number the morning after the night before and made a note of it. Then at least I could call him. Instead I was in limbo.

I was excruciatingly embarrassed about what had happened. Not once did I feel any sort of pleasure or satisfaction or fulfilment or love – the range of positive emotions you ought to feel after you've slept with someone for the first time. Instead, what seemed like a fantastic idea at the time had become a Hugely Terrible Thing that made me cringe whenever I thought about it, which was approximately every two seconds. It was made worse by the fact that Josh had made no effort to contact me since it happened. No *decent* person would get up and leave after a night of so-called passion without a cursory phone call to make sure you got home OK. Would they? But then, maybe Josh wasn't such a decent person after all. Maybe I'd been deluded by a nice bum and some smooth talk.

Or maybe I'd been deluded by myself.

Part of me felt I shouldn't care, that I should realize he was a rat and put it down to experience. But the trouble was, I *did* care. I'd been obsessed with Josh for months – he'd become my all-consuming passion. I'd never felt such an intensity of emotions over anyone else in my entire life. It was first love. Or lust. Or both. I couldn't let it end like this.

All those things he'd said – about wanting me, about fancying me – surely he meant them? Why else would he say them?

Perhaps he *had* been trying to get in touch with me. What if he'd lost my phone number? Maybe he'd been in an accident and was in hospital. Stranger things have happened. But no. Much as I wanted to believe all these things, much as I wanted everything to be OK, and to cling on to the silly dream where we got married, had loads of kids and lived Happy Ever After, something inside me told me to stop kidding myself. Something told me I'd made a great big whopper of a mistake. And it was up to me to sort it out.

I decided to take direct action. If I couldn't sort out my problems with Beth until she came home, at least I could try and sort out this thing with Josh. So instead of moping around the house hoping he'd stop by, and waiting by the phone just in case he called, I was going to have to put myself out of my misery and make a move. I was going to have to pay him a visit at home.

I felt calm and in control as I walked along the street where Josh lived, much more so than I'd expected. In a strange way, I felt like it wasn't me; there was another person who'd taken over my body for a couple of hours, an emotion-free alien, cold and dispassionate, a being looking for straight answers rather than someone whose mind had been befuddled by feelings and whose outlook was all misty-eyed and romantic. It made me feel stronger.

I walked purposefully up the path of his house and rapped on the door with my knuckles rather than using the buzzer. I waited. I rapped again. And waited. I pressed the buzzer several times and rapped at the same time. Still no answer. He wasn't in.

Damn you, Josh! I cursed as I started off down the street again. I was really hoping he'd be at home – it would have made this so much easier. Now I felt that in order to get this episode of my life over, I had to trawl the streets looking for him, which would be a whole lot trickier. At least if we were alone together I could shout and scream and throw things at him if I completely lost my cool. Mind you, I suppose I could do that in public too if I wanted to cause a scene. It might be quite entertaining to see his face as I tipped a pint of beer over his head. Or kicked him in the groin. Or rubbed his face in a plateful of spaghetti Bolognese. Or announced in a loud voice that he was useless in bed. OK, so I was fantasizing now – in reality I didn't think I'd do any of those things. Unless, of course, he *really* provoked me.

All I wanted was to know where I stood, to know if we were happening or just a one-night stand. That wasn't too much to ask, I felt, as I made my way to the Style Café, the second most likely place I thought I might find him.

I have to say I didn't feel terrifically comfortable walking through the doors of the Café. The last time I'd been here was when I was stood up by the dorky Todd. So to walk in on my own (again) and knowing that it was quite likely I'd be walking out on my own (again) didn't exactly fill me with glee.

Not that I should expect the staff to remember me. They'd probably had loads of people stood up in there since the bar had opened a few months back. They probably took bets with each other as to which people were the most likely to leave on their own at the end of each night. Not that I'm cynical or anything.

I walked up to the bar, my eyes roving the room as I did so. It was a busy weekday lunchtime, and the place was full of a real mish-mash of people: there were professional types in suits having business lunches, casually dressed shoppers stopping off for a sit-down over a coffee, and groups of local college kids hugging their mineral water and hoping to stay all after-noon. But there was no sign of Josh.

I was just about to leave when I caught sight of a group of lads at the far corner of the bar. There were about five of them. They had suddenly become quite loud and raucous which was what made me take notice of them, and Josh was among them. He had his back to me but I knew it was him because I could hear his voice blaring out. As I drew a few steps nearer I was convinced I heard my name mentioned. Surely not?

Other than Josh, I didn't recognize any of the faces. Oh, hang on – there was Gavin sitting side-on to me, listening to Josh talking. About me. I was rooted to the spot, horrified by what I was hearing. . .

"So there we were, practically getting down to

it on the sofa, when it's like she's suddenly remembered that I'm going out with her best friend and she goes all conservative on me." He broke off and took a glug of beer from the bottle he was holding. I felt the colour drain from my face as I listened to him carry on.

"Tells me that she can't possibly have sex with me while I'm going out with her mate. So I told her we'd finished, and that was it! She was all over me like a rash!" He laughed and they all joined in, slapping their thighs and guzzling beer, ears eager for the next snippet of gossip.

"So the minute Beth's back is turned, she's in there. I could hardly believe my luck!"

Angry tears welled up in my eyes and I felt physically ill by what I was hearing. I hadn't thought the situation could get much worse, but God, was I wrong! To see with my own eyes Josh broadcasting something so private to anyone who'd listen absolutely sickened me.

I stifled an anguished sob as I stood there, undecided as to whether I should face up to Josh or turn round and flee. Then Gavin looked up and caught my eye, his face registering a look of total shock as he realized I must have heard everything. I wasn't going to hang around to face any more humiliation though. I ran from the bar and into the street.

I fled down the road and round the nearest corner, where I stood huddled in a doorway for a while, gasping sobs coming from inside me. I was mortified. This was terrible – much worse than I could ever have expected.

I could just imagine the kind of things people would be saying about me once word got around. My reputation would go through the floor. It made my blood boil. How could Josh do this to me? He must hate me to be so cruel. Why? Why would he want to hurt me so much?

Suddenly everything Josh had ever said to me became meaningless. My feelings obviously meant nothing to him. Honesty and truth and emotions were just words to be abused. I no longer had any reason to believe him when he'd told me it was over between him and Beth. It was just a game he'd been playing with me.

My thoughts came back to Beth for the millionth time in the last few days. Poor Beth! Soon the whole town would know about this awful betrayal. I headed for home, determined to write a letter of confession to her. I would put it through her letterbox ready for when she got back. I owed her an explanation and I felt that the best way to get my thoughts out in a coherent form was to write them down. It was something I always did when I was faced with a problem concerning someone else. More often than not, I never sent these outpourings of my emotions, but writing about my predicament usually helped me get my feelings into some kind of orderly manner.

As soon as I got home I went straight to my bedroom and sat at my desk. Taking a couple of sheets of notepaper from a drawer, I began composing a letter to Beth.

Dear Beth, I began,
I know this is the coward's way out, but I haven't got the guts to tell you to your face. You see, while you were on holiday I slept with Josh. . .

Oh no! I thought bleakly. That sounds terrible. Ripping the paper up, I scrunched it into a tight ball and hurled it at the wall. Those few words, *While you were on holiday I slept with Josh* – they sounded so casual, like I was saying while you were on holiday I had a pizza and it was really nice.

Of course, the reality was much more devastating. I mean, fancying your best friend's boyfriend would be bad enough, snogging him would be unforgivable, but *sleeping* with him? That was unthinkable. And I'd done all three.

Poor Beth! She didn't deserve such disloyalty. Some friend I'd turned out to be!

I searched desperately for solutions. I knew it was a long shot but maybe, by some miracle, she wouldn't find out. I mulled over the prospect of keeping such a huge, black secret like that to myself for the rest of my life. It wouldn't be too much of a problem so long as Beth never uttered Josh's name again . . . and we never saw him again. Then I could stuff the awful incident into a little compartment in the shadowy depths of my mind, close the door on it, and (hopefully) never think of it again. But this was pretty unlikely. I had to face reality. Long shots were out. I had to tell her.

But somehow, sitting down and writing a letter to her seemed, well, a bit spineless. And OK, so I *am* a bit of a wimp when it comes to confrontation and getting the truth out into the open. I'd always wait for a guy to make the first move, or to tell me he loved me before I'd reciprocate. And I've never been able to hang my dirty washing out like some people can. I'm constantly amazed by the type of people who go on American chat shows like *Ricki Lake* or *Oprah*, and stand there ranting about their private life – *really* personal stuff – knowing that millions of people across the world are tuning in with ghoulish glee. And that the next time they're in their local washeteria, people will be nudging each other and going, "There – that's the woman who had five lovers on the go but who ran off with her local vicar." That sort of stuff is beyond me.

So while I realized it would be easier for me to shove a note through Beth's door ready for when she came home from her holiday, I wasn't sure it mightn't only make matters worse. There she'd be, all tanned and refreshed, keen to see her boyfriend and friend, and what does she find on the mat under the letterbox? A scrawled message saying that she's been betrayed by the two people closest to her. Then what? I couldn't bear to think about what would happen next.

No, much as the thought filled me with dread, I owed it to her to tell her face to face.

The phone rang, dragging me from my cloud-sodden gloom of despair. Damn! I really couldn't be bothered to answer it – I wasn't in the mood. But since I was the only one at home I didn't have much choice. Hurling the pen across the desk in front of me, I looked up and scowled at the hunched-up body in the mirror. It glowered back, a picture of misery.

I hauled myself up, dived on to my bed and reached for the telephone extension on the bedside table. Sighing heavily, I picked up the receiver and put on my grumpiest, most unfriendly voice.

"Hello."

"Mel, it's me! I'm back!"

My stomach lurched at the sound of Beth's voice. In a split second my mind whirred into overdrive: what was she doing home? She wasn't due back from Wales yet. Why had she come back early? She must have heard about me and Josh. No, don't be stupid, she sounds *cheerful* for God's sake! She'd be at my front door spitting nails if she'd heard.

I quickly dragged my thoughts back to the present. My tongue was swelling to twice its normal size and was clinging to the roof of my dry mouth. No surprise then that my voice croaked as I spoke.

"Oh, er . . . Beth! Hi! Um, how was the holiday?"

"Brilliant. Just excellent, I had the best time ever. . ."

She babbled on but I wasn't listening. I felt completely wretched. I'd done something totally stupid and I knew I was going to lose my closest friend because of it. My heart was racing, thumping wildly. "You've got to tell her! You've got to tell her!" it boomed, bursting to get out of my body, desperate to alleviate the guilt. Tears began to prick the backs of my eyes.

"Look, Beth," I cut her off sharply, unable to

cope with the pretence that everything was all right. I was suddenly desperate to unburden myself.

I took a deep breath and spoke. "I've got to see you as soon as possible. There's something important I have to tell you. . ."

Chapter 10

Once I'd blurted out my spur-of-the-moment demand to see Beth, I was determined to get our meeting over and done with – what was the point in prolonging the agony? I suggested she meet me at a bar on the other side of town later that evening. She kept trying to get my news out of me: Had I met a guy? Was I in love? I wasn't pregnant, was I? I refused to be drawn, and just prayed that she wouldn't bump into anyone eager to pass on the awful gossip about me and Josh in the meantime.

The bus journey there was the most miserable imaginable. I could hardly bear to think about what I was going to say to Beth, let alone predict what her reaction would be. The best I could hope for was for Beth to hear the whole story, then *perhaps* she might be able to forgive me. Though I doubted it.

I tried turning the tables, imagining her coming to me and telling me that she'd slept with my boyfriend. I'd be livid. I think any friendship would be hard pushed to overcome that one.

The place we were meeting at was at the opposite end of the spectrum to the Style Café. It was situated down a back street in a deeply unhip part of town. From the outside it looked fairly inconspicuous with its permanently steamed-up windows and garish-looking transfers of hot dogs and beefburgers stuck all over them.

But the inside was something else. The owners must have had some kind of connection with America because the place was heaving with original US memorabilia, and all the beers, food and even chocolate bars and sweets had their origin in the States. Plus (and this was the reason Beth and I went there, but only as a special treat) they served the most scrummy tasting hot chocolate ever – it was literally like drinking a liquid Galaxy bar.

When I arrived, food and drink were the last things on my mind. As I crossed the road in front of the bar, I could just make out Beth through a fugged-up window. She was sitting at a table overlooking the bleak street outside. She gave me a broad grin and waved frantically when she saw me.

I went inside and she stood up and threw her arms around me in a big hug, which made me feel even worse.

"It's so good to see you!" she said. "I've got loads to tell you. And I can't wait to hear your big news."

I cringed inside at these words. I wished a big hole would appear in the floor and swallow me up so I wouldn't have to face up to my actions. Sadly, it didn't and I was forced to carry on.

"Do you want another hot chocolate?" I said, noticing her half-empty mug, putting off the inevitable.

"No, thanks," she said. "One's enough. You get one though. I'll stay here and save our seats."

"Won't be a tick," I said and hurried off to the bar, glad to escape for a few more seconds, terrified to get too intimate because I knew that soon she was going to regret hugging me.

While my order was being prepared I skulked off to the loo to try and calm myself. My hands were shaking and I took deep breaths to try and stop my insides from churning up. I wondered if there was any way I could chicken out of telling her at such a late stage. But there wasn't. I had to go through with it.

Those few stolen moments were to prove very expensive, as I realized when I re-entered the café and saw Dee and another girl standing at Beth's table. *Oh, no!* I thought. *Dee has to be the biggest gossip in college.* I was sure that if anyone knew what had gone on between me and Josh, she would.

I stood at a distance, watching closely, trying to work out what they were saying to each other. Why were Dee's arms waving about with great gusto as she spoke? As I walked back on to the scene I knew why.

As soon as she caught sight of me, Beth's face contorted into a look of pure outrage.

"So that's your big news, is it?" she seethed. Dee's head snapped round in my direction. Realizing who it was, she wrinkled her nose and made a face like she'd just stepped in something unpleasant. She turned back to Beth, patted her on the arm, murmured something like "I'll leave you to it", and rushed away to the other side of the café, gliding past me silently but with great flourish. Her friend – a girl I'd never seen before – gave a similar sneer and followed suit.

It was obvious that she'd told Beth. I was dismayed that she had heard it from someone other

than me. There was even less chance of her for-
giving me now.

"It *is* true then? About you and Josh." Her face
was a mixture of hate and hurt.

"I can explain," I said.

"You don't need to explain. It's already been
explained to me. In great detail." She spat the
words out, venom in her voice.

"Please," I begged, "listen to me for a minute.
You don't understand—"

She cut me off. "Understand?" she shrieked.
"You slept with my boyfriend the minute my
back's turned. What more is there to understand?"

"But it wasn't like that," I pleaded. "Josh told
me you'd split up."

"So that makes it all right?" Her voice was
becoming increasingly hysterical, her eyes were
bulging. "That makes you think I'm going to
welcome you with open arms, kiss you on the
cheek and wish you both the best of luck? Get
real, Mel. For your information – and not that I
owe it to you to tell you anything – as far as I
was concerned Josh and I were still going out.
Though we're obviously not any more."

So he was lying. Bastard!

"You've got to hear me out," I begged her.
"You've got to give me a chance."

Her face had coloured red with anger now, and her lips were set in an icy sneer as she spoke. "Get lost, Melanie! You don't *deserve* a chance. I hate you for this. I'll never forgive you."

She stood up, grabbed her bag, pushed past me and bolted through the door and out of my life.

I was too numb to cry, too confused to think straight. I didn't know what to do for the best. I wanted to be able to blame someone else – if I could somehow make myself the victim, everything would be fine again. The trouble was, I *did* only have myself to blame. OK, so Josh had a hand in this, but he hadn't forced me to sleep with him. I was his willing partner in crime, though I now found it hard to believe I'd been prepared to risk everything for such a lowlife as him.

However much he'd lied to me, Josh wasn't accountable for what had happened between Beth and me. But he was responsible for dragging my name down to his amoebic level, and I wasn't going to let him get away with it. I felt I had the right to some kind of explanation for his actions. And I had an overpowering urge to seek revenge.

I decided to stay out of Beth's way for a day or so in the hope that she would calm down a little, enough to let me at least speak to her. But Josh? Josh I had to deal with now.

I decided to call on him at home again, and this time I'd camp out all night to see him if I had to. Fortunately, I didn't have to take such drastic measures, because as I walked into his road I saw him open the door of his house and step outside, as though he was about to leave.

"Hey, Josh!" I shouted. I started running towards him, only stopping when I was a metre or so away, meeting him halfway up his path.

He looked at me. Then his face broke out into that same smile I'd seen so many times before. Only now it had lost its earlier appeal – it had become smarmy as opposed to knowing, lecherous instead of winning.

"Hello, Mel," he smirked. "What brings you here?"

"Don't pretend you don't know, you lying swine! I've seen Beth, and not surprisingly she won't have anything to do with me."

He looked a little shocked. "She's back from her holiday then? I didn't realize. But look, Mel, you can't stand there and tell me you're surprised."

"No," I agreed, "but she did tell me that you

hadn't broken up with her before she went away. You lied to me, and I could kill you for it."

"Hey, steady on," he said, amazed at my outburst. "I didn't make you do anything you didn't want to. And, to my mind, Beth and I were finished. Even if I didn't tell her before she went away, I was going to tell her as soon as she got back."

"So why did you lie to me? Why did you tell everyone? Why are you out to destroy my life?" I had so many questions that demanded answers, they were all spilling out at once.

He looked at me like I was mad, and said, "Don't you think you're being a bit over-dramatic?"

"Not at all," I replied. "I've lost my friendship with Beth. I've lost all respect—"

"Oh, come on!" he exclaimed, exasperated. "You were gagging for it. You made that obvious from the start. And you got what you wanted. So what's the problem?"

"The problem is that you then broadcast it to the whole world. Why did you do that? It was between us, no one else." My voice had gone up an octave by now, my fingernails were digging into the palms of my hands and the anger inside me was bubbling to the surface. I could not believe the audacity of the guy.

142

"Look, I'm sorry about that," he said, soothing tones in his voice. "I'd had a few beers. I hadn't meant to say anything but we were having this conversation about girls and it just seemed appropriate at the time to mention it. I got a bit carried away – guys do things like that. But I certainly didn't mean for you to overhear. Gavin told me you had. I'm genuinely sorry about that." His face took on a totally false look of deep regret and he went to put a comforting arm around my shoulder.

"Look," he cooed. "I'm just about to go out, or I'd invite you in for a coffee. Some other time, perhaps?"

I couldn't believe it! He was actually trying to win me round with his smooth talk. I felt like punching his lights out, the creep!

I shook his arm away from me.

"You must be joking!" I spat. "I can't believe I ever fell for you. This sounds pathetic now, but I really liked you and I thought you liked me. I wasn't after a one-night stand."

"And it needn't be," he slimed. "Look, I'm truly sorry about mouthing off in front of my mates like that – I shouldn't have done it. But we can still see each other, can't we? We can have a bit of fun together—"

"A bit of fun?" I broke in. "Is that all I am to

you? *A bit of fun?* No way, Josh. You can go and get *a bit of fun* elsewhere. You're a liar and a cheat and you've got a big mouth. Why on earth would I want to have anything more to do with you?"

He looked down at the floor, feigning hurt. "Well, I'm sorry you feel like that. Maybe we should call it a day then."

"What about Beth?" I yelled at him. "Are you going to see her, speak to her?"

"Somehow I don't think she'll want to speak to me if she knows what's been going on."

"Don't you think you owe her an explanation?" I raged.

"Not really. What I said to you was true – she and I weren't going anywhere."

"What you really mean is you haven't got the guts to face up to her. You're pathetic, Josh. I wish I'd never laid eyes on you."

"Well, that's easily solved," he said, striding past me down the path. "If you're sure that's how you feel, I'll just get out of your way and we'll forget about it, eh?"

And with that he stomped off down the road while I stood open-mouthed, watching him until he was out of sight. I suddenly felt my legs go all wobbly so I had to sit on his front garden wall, too stunned to move after what had just happened.

What a prat! I thought. How on earth did I fall for such a prize wally? The guy was unreal. He didn't give two hoots about Beth or me — all he was interested in was his own enjoyment. He was obviously only out for himself. He didn't care about other people's feelings, so long as he had a good time. I could hardly believe I'd fallen for the flannel, or that Beth had too.

It was difficult for me to believe that just a week ago I had thought I was in love with Josh. I laughed bitterly to myself at the way things had turned out. I had been totally taken in by him, and had completely deluded myself into thinking we were love's young dream. How stupid could anyone be?

I was so engrossed in my thoughts that I didn't notice the shadowy figure standing over me, until I heard someone clear their throat rather obviously. I looked up, squinting into the sunlight. Oh no! It was Gavin. Gavin, who knew all about my sex life, thanks to Josh. My face turned pink with humiliation at the sight of him. What was he going to think, seeing me sitting here on Josh's wall like a ridiculous love-struck schoolgirl?

"Hello, Mel," he said. "How are you?"

"As well as can be expected for someone whose life is over," I replied morosely. "If you're looking for Josh, he's not here," I added.

"Oh," he said. "D'you know where he's gone?"

"Timbuktu, hopefully," I said through gritted teeth.

"Oh." He paused. "Are you OK?" He looked quizzically at me sitting there, in utter gloom.

Poor Gavin! It wasn't his fault his friend was a jerk.

"Sorry," I said, relenting a little. "I'm fine. I really don't know where Josh has gone. He went off in that direction (pointing) about ten minutes ago."

I stood up and smiled feebly. "Anyway, I'm off home. See you, Gavin."

"Er, I'll walk with you," he said quickly. "I'm going that way."

"Are you sure you want to be seen with me?" I challenged, eyebrows raised. "I mean, I can't exactly be held in high esteem around here at the moment, not after Josh put the boot in at the Style Café the other day."

"If it's any consolation, I haven't told anyone. Josh was well out of order bragging like that. He had no right."

"Try telling him that!" I muttered. I then found myself relating some of the conversation I'd just had with Josh, ending by explaining that I couldn't believe how he seemed to be able to walk all over my and Beth's feelings without any qualms whatsoever.

That was what hurt the most – that and the fact that we'd had no idea what he was really like, I said.

Gavin looked right back at me and said urgently, "You're not still hung up on him are you?"

"God, no!" I spluttered. "No way! But, well, you probably know him as well as anyone. And I keep wondering why you never said anything about him to me when you knew my best friend was involved with him."

"I suppose it's because it's none of my business," he replied curtly. "And anyway, if you remember rightly I did try and warn you that he was a bit of a lad that night we all went rollerblading. It's not my fault that you chose not to heed it."

We walked along in silence for a while. Of course he *had* said something, however cryptic it was at the time. Just think – none of this need have happened if I'd listened to him instead of letting lust get in the way. And if I hadn't been so obsessed with Josh, I could be going out with a nice guy now – someone like Gavin.

Amazing thing, hindsight.

"You and Josh seem to be so different," I conceded, thinking aloud. "What I don't understand is how you can still be friends with him, knowing what he's like. I mean, why do you have anything to do with him?"

Gavin shoved his hands deep into his trouser pockets, and walked along the road, deep in thought. It must have been a full twenty seconds that felt like twenty minutes before he spoke again.

"We go back a long way," he started. "When we were kids we were like brothers. We're both only children, and I suppose I looked up to him. He's always been dead cool – good at sports, quick-witted, good-looking, and much more confident than me. I envied him for all that and in a funny way I wanted to be like him. I was always too sensible, too concerned about doing well at school, always a month behind the trends, whereas he was at the cutting edge. But even though we were so different we got on.

"His parents split up when he was nine or ten and he took it really badly. Even though it wasn't his fault, he's always blamed himself for it. He became quite withdrawn for a while and a lot of people were worried about him. Then he seemed to get over it and went to the other extreme. He started hanging out with a rough crowd of kids, smoking and getting drunk, then he started bunking off school and began knocking about with lots of different girls. He became a bit of a stud, treated girls so badly that they wouldn't take any more and dumped him. We began to drift apart a bit after that.

"It sounds really swotty but I wanted to get good grades to go to university, whereas he was happy to drift and bum about. He left school at sixteen, while I went on to sixth form college, and although we still hung out together, it was more like once a week rather than every night. He's someone I used to know better than anyone else in the world but who's slowly becoming like a complete stranger to me. . ."

His voice trailed off, and he stopped in his tracks and stood looking at the reflection of himself in the window of the shoe shop we were passing. He looked perplexed.

"Weird, isn't it," he said eventually, "how you can be so close to someone and think, really *believe*, that they'll be a part of your life for ever? Then, something happens and you fall out. Or not even that – you might just gradually grow apart, then – boom! – a few years down the line and it's like you don't know them at all."

His words went straight through me, slicing into my heart and ripping out the other side. He was so right. What he was saying applied so much to me and Beth, it was uncanny. Except that the catalyst in our relationship wasn't a parent walking out, it was my betrayal with Josh.

I'd never imagined going through life without having Beth somewhere in the picture, even if it was at the end of a telephone line because she'd married a sheep farmer and emigrated to Australia. Or something. I always thought we'd be there for each other, giggling at our crap jokes, getting up to all sorts of mischief through-out our lives together, being aged eighty and reminiscing about our carefree youth.

Now there was nothing. No future for us. I felt like I wasn't a whole person any more, I'd been cut in half, one part left to carry on while the other withered and died.

I began to sob, silently at first as I walked along, staring at the ground, hoping that Gavin wouldn't notice. Then, when I found that because I was trying to stifle the sobs I couldn't breathe any more, I started to gulp air into my lungs. Which made things worse because I suddenly had to let go and this terrific howl came from inside me and I stopped in the middle of the street and just . . . wailed.

Gavin paused and turned to look at me like I was a strange animal from another planet.

"Oh no!" he cried. "What on earth is the matter?"

I stood there, not daring to look at him and desperately rummaging in my bag for a tissue to stop the flow of mascara running down my cheeks. Gulping more air in an effort to breathe, I tried to speak, but could make no sense of the sounds coming from my mouth. Gavin carefully steered me towards a wooden bench by the side of the road and we sat there for a few moments, him patting my hand and me trying to gather my thoughts.

Once I was fairly sure I could string a sensible sentence together I told him the whole story of me and Josh, from the first time I laid eyes on him at the Style Café right up to the slanging match we'd just had in the street. And I went to great lengths to make sure he knew that Josh wasn't the reason I was crying, as I then went into detail about the huge rift that I'd made between me and Beth. And when I'd finished spilling my guts on the pavement in front of me, I felt hugely better, like two great big boulders that had been sitting on my shoulders had been lifted.

I was a bit shocked at myself – I'd never expected to unload the so-called "emotional baggage" psychologists are always going on about on to Gavin of all people. I hardly knew him, but he'd suddenly gone from being the pain in the bum bloke who had once fancied me (though not any more, I was sure) to my greatest confidant. Strange.

Throughout it all he sat, nodding, but saying nothing. When he was confident I'd finished, he leapt to his feet and pulled me up alongside him.

"Come on," he said taking hold of my elbow and steering me in the opposite direction from that which we'd been travelling.

"Where are we going?" I said, a little startled by his sudden activity.

"To see Beth," he announced decisively. "We're going to sort this mess out once and for all."

Chapter 11

"I'm not sure this is such a good idea," I wailed pathetically as I trailed a few paces behind Gavin. "Maybe we ought to give her a while longer to calm down."

"Don't be so ridiculous," he scolded. "Give her much more time and the rot will have *really* set in. She'll have imagined you into a vicious two-headed monster by then, and you'll never get her to listen to you. She'll have had loads of other friends offering tea and sympathy too and she'll have decided she doesn't need you anyway."

He was right, and I was being a wimp. The thought of facing up to Beth made me feel quite ill. Even having Gavin playing on my team didn't make me feel any less sick. I guessed the best attitude to have was expect nothing and hope I'd be pleasantly surprised.

"Have you thought about what you're going to say?" he asked as we neared Beth's.

"Er, not really," I answered. "I keep having visions of a replay of the last conversation we had, except this time she's holding a frying-pan in her hand and bashing me over the head with it."

He laughed. "Why don't you let me do most of the talking then, and you can chip in every now and again? There might be more chance of her listening to me, an impartial observer of the situation."

"Ooh yes, that's a much better idea," I said, the relief in my voice obvious.

Gavin strode up to Beth's house and rang the bell. I stood next to him, biting my nails nervously. Beth's mum's face took on a slightly frosty look as she opened the door and saw it was me standing there.

"Beth's not in," she announced brusquely. "She's gone away for a few days."

"Oh," I said. "Do you know when she'll be back?"

"I'm not sure."

"Oh."

I didn't know what else to say, so Beth's mum

brought the exchange to a close by continuing, "I'm not sure she wants to see you at the moment, Mel, but I'll tell her you called." She looked stony-faced as she withdrew inside and shut the door on us.

"Thanks," I said weakly to the closed door and skulked off down the path.

I was glad to have Gavin with me to make some sensible decisions. "Look," he said, "I'll tell you what we'll do. I'll try calling her in a couple of days and when I get hold of her, I'll arrange to meet. I won't say anything about you coming, but if you tag along too we'll take it from there."

"I wonder where she's gone?" I was half-listening to Gavin but my mind was running away with itself. Something didn't quite add up. Firstly, Beth had come home from her holiday a day early. And then she'd disappeared off again. Why?

I could only guess at the reasons for her odd movements. She could have had a row with her family, which would account for her coming home. But she was the type of person to spill the beans to anyone who'd listen, and she'd seemed quite cheerful when she rang me on her return. As to her current disappearance, I could only put that down to her wanting to get away from the gossip. And from me.

But this was all conjecture – I'd have to hold tight for a while and wait for the next chapter in the ongoing saga to unfold.

When Gavin invited me to go for a coffee with him, I politely declined. Mentally I was exhausted – I just wanted to go home and lie low. These last couple of days had been a barrage on my emotions, I needed time to recuperate and contemplate.

I thanked Gavin for having a shoulder big enough for me to cry on, asked him to call me as soon as he'd spoken to Beth, and, not for the first time, left him standing outside my front door.

I was on tenterhooks for the next two days. Knowing how gossip and rumour had a tendency to spread through our small town I didn't dare leave the house in case I bumped into someone who'd heard Josh mouthing off about me and him. Instead, I paced up and down, planning over and over again what I was going to say to Beth, jumping with fright every time the phone rang in case it was Gavin with my summons.

I spent a lot of time reminiscing. I dug out old photo albums and chuckled at an endless stream of memories. There was one shot in particular that made me laugh out loud. It was an old school photo of just the two of us sitting at a beat-up wooden desk, grinning like lunatics into the camera lens. We must have been five or six and we each wore puff-sleeved dresses and had ribbons in our hair. We had cheeky faces and looked all the more ridiculous as we'd both lost an upper front milk tooth, giving our smiles a slightly surreal quality, like we'd deliberately blacked them out. Even at that young an age you could see Beth's natural beauty shining through.

There were some ludicrous pictures of us in bizarre poses – in fancy dress at a party held at our local pub, me got up like a farmer with Beth as my pet pig. I remember I had her on a lead all night, and she oinked at anyone who'd listen. And there was a photo that I remember we'd ceremoniously ripped in half when we'd fallen out with the girl at the other end of the picture. Her face had been cut into tiny pieces and thrown in the bin. We both felt bad when we all made up a few weeks later.

I also had a keepsake box that contained sentimental stuff from my life, and as I rooted through it I was surprised at how much of it was devoted to events that I'd shared with Beth. There were Blur and Oasis concert tickets from years ago that I'd saved as souvenirs, funny letters and cards, photos of us at karaoke nights, postcards from holidays abroad. Each item triggered off a memory, usually good, sometimes cringe-making, and nearly always funny – in retrospect if not at the time.

Now I felt an overwhelming sadness as I sifted through the years. It suddenly dawned on me how much I took Beth for granted, how I assumed she'd always be there with me to enjoy the good times and help me get through the bad. Now, when we both had to face the very worst of times, who could have predicted that I would be the cause of them and my very best friend the sufferer?

When Gavin finally rang I felt relief that the waiting was over, mixed with apprehension at the prospect of what might happen next. Gavin said Beth had been keen to talk to him. They'd arranged to meet at the Style Café one lunchtime, which made me feel even odder, as that was the place where all our troubles had begun. My name had not been mentioned during their conversation. I wasn't entirely surprised.

By the time I arrived at the Café, I was jittering with nerves. I walked straight past the place and had to stand round the corner taking deep breaths for five minutes to put myself back on an even keel. Then I gathered myself together and walked in.

I saw them straight away. Beth was sitting with her back to me, while Gavin was facing in my direction. He looked animated, as though he was going into great detail about something. Then he caught my eye as I made my way towards them. He shut up and stood up.

"Mel, hi!" he exclaimed like I was his long-lost sister. I managed to force a smile through my terror and looked from him to where Beth was sitting. The expression on her face was one of total horror. Her steely gaze turned from me to Gavin.

"You planned this, didn't you?" she said, then took her bag from the table and stood up as if to leave.

"Don't go, Beth," I pleaded. "If the last twelve years have meant anything to you, then please hear me out." My voice faltered as I finished, my desperation was so apparent.

She looked at me through frosty blue eyes, replaced her bag on the table, and sat down, arms folded defensively across her chest, a look of haughty disdain on her face.

Gavin plonked himself on a stool, while I grabbed hold of the back of the remaining chair for support, not daring to feel comfortable enough to sit myself.

"Go on," she commanded.

"I . . . um, well, I don't know how much Gavin has told you," I began, searching wildly for a good place to start, one that perhaps was marginally less incriminating than any other, "but the thing is this. I know I've done something terrible, and I don't really expect you to forgive me, but if you'll let me give you my side of the story, then I just hope it'll make you hate me slightly less."

My voice wobbled as I spoke, and I had trouble keeping my eyes from filling with tears. But something I said must have appealed to her, because Beth looked down at the table, and said quietly, "Get on with it, then."

I told her everything, the complete truth, from that first ill-fated meeting we'd both had with Josh, onwards and downwards to getting drunk and sleeping with him, to facing the bleak reality of what I'd done. The whole story, along with my full range of emotions, was laid bare. I was brutally honest with myself as well as with her.

I told her that I'd been jealous of her relationship with Josh, that I sometimes felt like an ugly duckling next to her, and that I envied her her self-confidence. But I also emphasized how much she meant to me, how I loved her and valued her as a person and how much I regretted messing up our friendship. At the end of my exposé I was left feeling completely drained.

Beth listened, said nothing, but watched my face intently the whole time I was talking. When I finally stopped splurging my feelings all over her, I slumped heavily into the seat I'd been cowering behind. Eventually she spoke.

"Well, as you've been honest with me, I'll be equally truthful," she said. "Although I told you the other day that Josh and I were still going out at the time I went on holiday, that wasn't strictly true. We had a huge row the night we all went rollerblading together. It was while me and Josh were still sitting in the car after you and Gavin had left to go home. I accused him of chatting up another girl while we were all waiting to go home from Rollerworld and he went ballistic. We ended up calling each other some terrible names.

"Although I'd been pretty happy up until then, there were a few discrepancies appearing in some of the things he said, and I was beginning to get a bit suspicious of him. The biggest problem was that I didn't trust him.

"Then he turned up as we were about to leave for Wales and we had another row. He told me I was a control freak who wanted to dictate his life, which was complete rubbish, so I broke it off between us.

"On the journey in the car I calmed down and decided that me going away would do us both good. It would give me time to think about where our relationship was going. When it got to Tuesday and I still wasn't missing him, I came to the conclusion that we were going nowhere, so I had no intention of trying to get back with him when I came home, anyway.

"Of course, in the meantime you and him . . . er . . . happened. And when Dee – who's got to have the biggest gob in the world – told me what you'd been up to, I saw red. I was humiliated more than anything. I could just imagine what people would think and say once they got to hear of it, which with Dee around wouldn't take long. I felt like such a mug.

"I wouldn't have been in the slightest bit surprised to come home and hear that Josh had been messing around with someone, but not you, Mel. You were the last person on my list. No, scrap that – you weren't on it at all.

"Then I figured that if you could jeopardize our friendship for a fling with Josh, then I couldn't mean that much to you. That's what hurt me the most. I couldn't believe that you were about to chuck (as you say) twelve years down the tube. It was beyond me.

"I was quite prepared never to speak to you

again, that's how much you hurt me. But sitting here and listening to you, and hearing what Gavin told me about what Josh is really like before you came in, has helped put it all into perspective.

"The fact that I know Josh hasn't tried to contact me since I got back makes me realize how lucky I was to get away from him when I did. God only knows what might have happened to me if I'd got involved any deeper!

"And the truth is, I actually think I've come off quite lightly compared to you. At least I never thought I was in love with him. OK, so I was besotted in the beginning, but I never really thought we'd end up together for ever. Not like you."

I gave her a wry smile and said, "Yeah, but I wasn't living in the real world, was I? I didn't know Josh very well so I created this fantasy guy in my head. That was who I fell for – someone who didn't exist. My mistake was getting him mixed up with the real person.

"I feel so stupid, like a schoolgirl who's fallen for her Maths teacher and built up this whole relationship between them in her head, only to find out he's happily married with three kids and just looks on her as a silly little giggly girl who's crap at calculus."

I saw the corners of Beth's mouth crease into the smallest of smiles. There were two weeny cracks on each side of her lips – hardly notice-able, but they were definitely there. Moments later, they were gone. For the first time since we'd been sitting here, I saw a flicker of hope. In the next breath Beth blew it out.

"I'm really glad Gavin did his Good Samaritan bit and got us together," she contin-ued. "I feel like it's helped clear the air between us. But don't expect too much of me, Mel. I *can* forgive you for what happened, but I don't know if I can ever forget it, or even if I can trust you again. It'll take time."

I stared hard at the cocktail list standing in the middle of the table next to the mini jukebox. It was cheerful and bright with little illustrations of overflowing glasses and champagne corks popping and smiley faces of people celebrating. It was *so* not how I felt at the present moment.

Of course, Beth was absolutely right. I could hardly expect her to welcome me back and immediately invite me out on the pull with her as though nothing had happened, could I? But the prospect of things never being the same again, and of our friendship moving on to a different, less intimate level, didn't make me feel any more optimistic than I had when I'd first walked in an hour ago.

Beth swiftly changed the subject. "I wonder where Gavin went to?" she mused.

The stool Gavin had been slumped on was indeed empty. We'd been so engrossed in conversation, neither of us had noticed he wasn't there any more. I stood up and went to the bar to see if he was getting a drink. But no, it was devoid of any life. Perhaps he was at another table, out of the way, or in the loo? The girl serving behind the bar smiled and passed me a note.

"From the guy who was with you," she said, still smiling. I unfolded the piece of white paper and read the scrawled message: *Hope it works out OK between you two. I feel surplus to requirements. See you around. Gavin.*

Oh. I was taken aback for a second but couldn't decide why. Then I worked out that I was disappointed that he'd gone. He'd been so kind to me, a real rock, and I enjoyed his company. I wondered if I'd see him again, then realized that I didn't even have his address or phone number. I knew very little about him at all, whereas he knew everything about me and my problems. So far, I hadn't shown any interest in him as a person whatsoever, and I felt quite bad about that.

When I got back to the table, Beth was on her feet, gathering her things together.

"I'm going to have to go," she said. "I'm meeting someone."

Normally she would have added a "Why don't you come along?" or "I'll ring you when I get home." But not any more. Things had already changed.

I smiled weakly and managed a quiet, "OK."

I was about to add that I'd phone her soon, but Beth beat me to it.

"Why don't you leave it to me to call you sometime?" she said.

Then she turned her back on me and walked out the door.

Chapter 12

Sometime later . . .

"Come on, Beth, hurry up! We'll be late."

I was lying sprawled on the bed watching my friend as she stood in front of her full-length mirror, a blue dress hooked over her left arm, a red one hooked over the right. She held each one up in front of her in turn, while she studied herself in the mirror and frowned.

"I don't know which one to wear," she sighed. "Which do you like?"

"The red," I said. Laughing, I added, "Definitely the red. It matches your eyes."

"Cow," she laughed, mock hatred in her voice. "Are you trying to tell me something?"

"Only that you can't expect to have anything other than red eyes if you stay out partying until four o'clock in the morning."

"God! You sound just like my mother," she scolded. "I think I will wear the red though. Or what about the black one I wore last Saturday? That might look better. I wonder where it is. . ."

"Beth!" I squawked. "Have you seen the time? We should have left ages ago."

"Won't be a sec," she muttered, clambering into the red dress.

While Beth buzzed around, hopelessly late as usual, I lay back on the bed and cogitated. It felt like old times again, I thought – Beth in a flap, and me moaning at her to get a move on. It was *almost* like nothing had ever gone wrong between us.

It had taken time for the bridge to be repaired. I didn't hear from Beth for ten days after our summit meeting in the Style Café, and while I was tempted every single day to pick up the phone and call, I knew in my heart that I needed to wait for her to make the first move. It was her decision. So when I did hear her voice at the other end of the line, cheerily asking how I was, I could have cried with relief right there and then.

We didn't have the easiest of conversations, and there were a couple of stilted silences as we both struggled for what to say next. She asked if

I wanted to go and see the new blockbuster film on at the Odeon, which was a fab idea. It was a comedy and as we've both got the same sense of humour I thought it would be a good icebreaker. I wasn't wrong – we had a brilliant time, although I remember no mention of guys being made during the evening, and the subject of Josh certainly never came up.

Our friendship began to get back into its stride, and eventually we began sharing jokes about the opposite sex. When Beth began making fleeting – disparaging – references to Josh, I knew we were on the mend.

This evening – if Beth ever managed to be ready enough to get out of the house, that is – was going to be very special to me. Firstly, I was going to meet Steve. He was Beth's new boyfriend. They'd met while she was on holiday in Wales and he was the main reason why she didn't care two hoots whether she and Josh got back together. Steve, Beth informed me enthusiastically, was The One. Also, according to her, he made Josh seem like Frankenstein's monster, both in looks and personality. Amazingly, Steve only lived in the next town so it wasn't likely to be the kind of holiday romance that turns into a long-distance disaster once you get home.

Steve was also the reason why Beth had come

back from her holiday early, as he had to get back to work in a flash designer menswear shop on the Saturday. He offered Beth a lift home on the back of his "throbbing" Harley Davidson, and she jumped at the chance. (Who wouldn't?)

Steve now took up a major part of Beth's life. He was her bolt-hole after she'd found out about me and Josh. He was the reason for her blood-shot eyes. And they'd even discussed marriage – something Beth always swore she wouldn't do before the age of thirty. It was serious stuff.

I felt like a major step in the right direction had been taken when Beth suggested I meet up with her and Steve for this night out. It seemed that perhaps she was beginning to trust me once more, whereas I'd expected her never to let me near any of her boyfriends again for fear that I might jump on them – though of course this could be my own paranoia.

The second reason this evening was going to be special to me was because of Gavin. I'd been keen to see him again after all the help he'd given me over Josh. I wanted to thank him for bringing Beth and me back together that day at the Style Café, but there was another reason: whenever I thought about him, I had a really weird feeling in my stomach which I couldn't quite put my finger on but which was sort of nice and cosy. I found myself thinking about him a lot.

I'd had no idea how to contact him, not knowing where he lived and not even being aware of any regular haunts he might frequent. So I'd had to pin everything on Beth in the hope that she might know of his whereabouts.

When she first rang me out of the blue, I didn't dare bring the subject of Gavin up, so it took a good while for me to pluck up courage to ask if she knew his phone number. Thankfully she did, and when she asked me why I needed it and I told her I wanted to see him again because I really liked him, she was genuinely pleased. That's when she suggested this night out as a foursome. When I admitted I wasn't sure Gavin would want to go out with me she bet me £10 that he'd say yes, which I thought was very loyal of her.

I prayed she was right and after I'd put the phone down to her I immediately picked it up again to phone Gavin. As I listened to it ringing, I couldn't think of a single reason why he would want to go out with me. I'd already rejected him once – worse than that I'd then slept with his friend and the whole town knew about it. But before I could chicken out and replace the receiver someone answered. It was him.

"G-G-Gavin, it's Mel," I stuttered like the pathetic moron I was. "I just called to . . . erm

. . . see how you were." God, that sounded pathetic! I thought.

There was a good hour's silence at the end of the line. It was probably more like three seconds but I was feeling a little over-sensitive. At last Gavin spoke.

"Mel!" he exclaimed, in obvious surprise. "Blimey, you're the last person I expected to hear from! How *are* you?" He sounded pleased – no, more than that – *delighted* that I'd called.

It gave me the confidence to carry on, and we gossiped like lifelong friends for absolutely ages. I filled him in on the situation between me and Beth – and Steve – and it turned out not to be any effort at all for me to invite him out with us. I gave a grin wider than the Thames Estuary when I heard him say he'd be thrilled to accept. There were no mind games being played and from what I could gather he seemed as keen to see me as I was to see him. I felt elated when I came off the phone, and was on a high for the rest of the day and well beyond.

I felt so comfortable I didn't even create a fuss for myself on the night of our date. There was no faffing over what to wear, no bad hair day traumas, and my make-up slid on first time. It only took me two hours to get ready. I'd surpassed myself!

We were all meeting at Millennium, a desperately trendy bar-cum-eating-place-cum-nightclub. It was where all the local kids went to let off steam and hang out. When Beth and I arrived there was no sign of Gavin, but I guessed Steve was here, because when she saw a guy sitting at a stool in the bar Beth ran up to him and threw her arms around his neck like she hadn't seen him for months, not a few hours as was the reality. They snogged furiously for ten minutes or so while I looked embarrassed and felt like I was surplus to requirements, then Beth managed to come up for air long enough to introduce us. He was charming and hip and confident and not my type at all. No, *really*.

We sat chatting for a while and I began to feel like a gooseberry. Then panic set in and I wondered if Gavin had forgotten or stood me up or something equally horrifying. I kept looking round the bar, which was where we said we'd meet, then I trawled the club on my own, searching every nook and cranny for a sighting of him. Nothing.

As I made my way dolefully back to where Beth and Steve were deep in conversation, I saw him walk through the door. Wow! I thought, stopping to watch him pick his way through clusters of people, his eyes sweeping this way and that, looking for a face he recognized. He looked divine! I was definitely seeing him in a new light.

I went over to him and he gave me the most gorgeous smile which made my pulse jump a beat and my heart spin cartwheels.

"Hello," I squeaked. "I thought you weren't coming."

"Sorry I'm late," he said. "I got held up. Actually, the truth is I spent so long getting ready I lost track of time." He laughed and his easy candour made me fall for him a little more. Butterflies the size of elephants were beating their wings in my tummy and my knees were starting to quiver with nervous anticipation.

I led him over to where the love-birds were sitting cooing at each other. When she saw us Beth stood up and kissed Gavin on the cheek and introduced him to Steve. We made chitchat for a while, then Steve and Beth got into a heavy conversation between themselves and Gavin and I bought drinks and sat down at a nearby table.

We hadn't been talking for long before Gavin brought up the only topic I was hoping to avoid.

"You know," he announced suddenly, "I knew you fancied Josh that night we all went rollerblading."

"Did you?" I exclaimed, shocked at his forth-rightness.

"Of course. It was so obvious, especially when you started pumping me for information about him on the way home. I was pig sick with envy that it was him you were interested in and not me."

"Oh no! I'm sorry," I cried. "I must have been so boring, but I was obsessed with him. God knows why."

He carried on. "I was incensed when he mouthed off about your 'night of passion' as he called it. I was jealous of him and I hated him for dragging your name through it. I thought he might be taking you for a ride, like he has with girls so many times before. I was so livid, we ended up nearly fighting in the street."

"No!" I said, aghast.

"Well, it wasn't just that," he continued. "I suppose it was getting towards the end of the line for us anyway, and him bragging was what tipped our friendship into the dumper."

"So why were you going to see him at his house that day you saw me on the wall? *she said nosily,*" I grinned.

"I wasn't," he smiled. "I was walking past the end of the road and I saw you. It was a good excuse to come up and talk to you."

175

"Oh." I blushed furiously, excited but also embarrassed at what I was hearing.

"So have you seen much of Josh since then?" I asked.

"I've seen him around, but so far I've managed to avoid actually getting into a conversation with him."

We fell silent, both speculating on the fate of Josh. I wondered whether he was at all remorseful for the hurt he'd caused in his selfish quest for entertainment. I doubted it.

My eyes came to rest on a guy standing alone at the other side of the bar. He looked a bit like Josh – a little rougher perhaps. Funny how a few months ago I would probably have made a move on him simply because he wasn't dissimilar to the so-called guy of my dreams. I watched him for a while, a warped smile on my face.

He was hunched over a bottle of beer from which he took rapid slugs so that it was empty after seven or eight mouthfuls. I saw him gesture to a man behind the bar to bring him another beer. There was something about his mannerisms that made my body turn to ice. It couldn't be . . . I must be imagining it. But the face, the way he was standing, even the clothes I recognized.

It *was* Josh!

I grabbed Gavin's arm and stifled a yelp.

"Look! Over there. It's Josh."

Gavin's gaze followed my startled look to where he was standing.

"I don't believe it!" I went on. "I hoped I'd never set eyes on him again."

"Are you OK?" he asked, concerned.

"I'm fine," I said. "I'm just a bit shocked at seeing him. He looks awful."

"I'm glad you said that, and not how *dreamy* he looks or whatever it is you girls say," he teased.

"No, he's not the dreamy one – that's you," I said, then, amazed that I was being so forward, I changed the subject, suddenly flustered.

"I must just warn Beth about him being here," I muttered, standing up far too quickly and knocking both our glasses over so that they clattered along the tabletop and bounced on to the floor, spilling drink all over Gavin in the process.

"Ooh, sorry!" I squealed, jumping back and thinking what a clumsy mare I was, and knocking my chair over in the process. Beth heard the noise and rushed over waving a couple of Kleenex she must have dug out of her bag, while Gavin sat grinning at me and making soothing noises about it being OK, and that his trousers were only £250 in the Armani sale anyway. I think he was joking but it still put me in more of a stew.

Beth sat at Gavin's feet mopping up his trouser leg while I tried to clean up the mess on the table and Steve ordered more drinks.

My head spun round as I heard a familiar voice behind me.

"Well, well, what have we here?"

I looked straight into the mocking leer of Josh. Beth spat out an expletive to the side of me.

"Very cosy, I must say," he hissed, looking at Gavin. "I see you've got your harem around you," he continued towards his ex-friend. "I thought *I* was supposed to be the tart around here. Even *I* wouldn't be found in a club with two girls at once, Gav. Shame they're both soiled goods."

Gavin burst out of his seat and squared up to Josh. They stood like prize fighters in a ring, waiting for the bell to sound. A little nerve at Gavin's temple was visibly pulsating. The tension on his face was obvious. Then, just as suddenly, his expression went blank, his face relaxed and he backed down. He turned to walk away.

"Do yourself a favour, Josh," he said, "and get out of here."

Seizing his chance, and swift as a panther,

Josh sprang at Gavin, knocked him to the ground, and began hitting him in the face, chest and stomach.

Beth started screaming, Steve came rushing over, and I picked up a chair and began hitting Josh with it. My efforts had as much effect as a gnat dive-bombing a bear, but at least I was trying.

Seconds later, five or six sumo wrestlers dressed in bow ties and dinner suits materialized from all corners and waded in, untangling the wreckage by shouting obscenities and tearing us all away from each other.

A pair of arms like hams were wrapped around me from behind and a hand with best butcher's sausages for fingers peeled the chair from my grasp and placed it on the ground away from the action. I was then lowered into the chair and ordered to stay there or I'd be in trouble. I did as I was told and watched as Josh was pulled from Gavin, kicking like a mustang and yelling his head off.

Four sumos surrounded Josh; each one grabbed a limb, then they lifted him off the floor and dragged him off, his body scraping along the carpet. The two remaining lugs hauled Gavin on to his feet and he stood there, dazed and dis-orientated, with bloodstains on his shirt and a cut above his left eye. Apart from that he looked surprisingly unscathed.

"Are you all right?" I asked, and got a nod and a slightly wonky smile for a reply.

Steve and I began picking up chairs and putting them back round the table as the bouncers stood watching us, looking to see if we were going to cause any more trouble.

"Are you going to throw him out then?" demanded Beth to one of them, pointing towards Josh's prostrate body being hauled away.

"Yes, and I'm throwing you lot out, too," he replied. "We don't want any trouble in this establishment. Now come on, I want you all out."

Beth began protesting but to no avail, and we were hustled towards the exit.

"You know, Mel, I can't believe we nearly lost our friendship over that jerk," Beth exploded. "You're worth a thousand of Josh. I'm so relieved we came to our senses, and I'm so glad I've still got you."

"Me too," I murmured, my eyes awash with tears.

In a spontaneous gesture that was to begin a new chapter in our friendship, she came over and threw her arms around my neck and we hugged like only best friends can.

* * *

After Beth and Steve had sped off into the proverbial sunset on his Harley, Gavin and I walked the short journey to my house, arm in arm. For the first time I began to feel a little nervous, anticipation mixed with trepidation about what might happen next. Or – more worryingly – not.

As we got to my front door he stopped, untangled his arm from mine and scratched his head, a perplexed look on his face.

"Ah yes," he chuckled. "This is the door I know so well. I seem to remember being left on this side of it on several occasions. Are you going to abandon me here tonight like you normally do?" His eyes were laughing at me, his voice poking fun.

I recalled the previous two occasions when Gavin had walked me home, and how I'd scurried away on reaching my house, keen to seek sanctuary inside. This time it was so very different – now I didn't want the evening to end.

"We'll see," I teased, though I already knew the answer. As I turned to face him, he put his arms around me and pulled me towards him. Then we kissed – the most explosive, tender, wonderful kiss imaginable – and I realized that the evening needn't ever end, not if we didn't want it to. This was only the beginning.

Look out for other Confessions in this
revealing series.

"She's here," I practically whimpered.

"Who?" asked Laurie, confused.

"The wicked witch of the west," said Lewis.

"Oh, you mean *Faith*," Laurie nodded at him,
knowingly.

"Laurie, that's it – I'm leaving. I've just got bad
vibes about tonight."

Lewis and Laurie started in with protests. They
were both being brilliant, and here I was, such a
rotten mate I hadn't even bothered introducing
them to each other properly. I didn't have the
energy for niceties right at this point.

They persuaded me that I had to stay, so I took
the easy way out and agreed, then said that I
was going to the loo, secretly planning to nip
upstairs afterwards, find my jacket and shoot off.
I didn't want to mess up Laurie's night and make
her feel like she had to leave too, but a house full
of posh people I didn't know, a bloke who'd
gone all weird on me, and the gloom I felt

at knowing Faith was around just didn't bode well.

Who cared if it was Saturday night? Right at this point the thought of cuddling up on the old sofa in Rob's room with a corny late-night movie and a packet of tortilla chips sounded like absolute heaven.

Whoever was in the loo was taking for ever. I was on the point of heading off to find the bathroom upstairs (if Brown Owl hadn't cordoned it off already), when the door finally opened and out poured two giggling girls – Faith and her mate Emma.

"Oh, what an expected treat!" Faith said drily, her smile instantly gone and replaced with a stony expression. "What brings you here, Conk? Fed up of relying on middle-aged men and dodgy nightclubs for your social life?"

I tried to push past her into the loo, but she put out her arm and wouldn't let me through. Instead, I stared at the ground and tried to work out a response. All that came to my mind was to tell her that Mikey was only twenty-five, but that wasn't going to get me anywhere.

"I'm here with my mate. Leave me alone."

"Gee! This promises to be interesting."

"What do you mean?"

"Well, let's face it, your choice in friends isn't exactly sound, is it?" smirked Faith.

"There's nothing wrong with Laurie!"

"I wasn't talking about your hippy chick mate – it's just that I've heard you've been getting very chummy with the school's top slag."

For a second I was confused, then the realization of what she was getting at dawned on me; she was talking about Sam.

"There's nothing wrong with Sam!" I blurted out. It wasn't like I knew the girl all that well, but one thing I knew for sure – there was a lot more to her than her dodgy reputation.

"Oh, sure. Tell you what, let's have a little poll of everyone here – most of whom aren't even *at* our school – and see how many have heard about Sam the Slapper and her reputation. And you'd better be careful, Conk," she leant closer and I could smell the booze fumes on her breath, "people will start to see you the same way if you keep hanging out with her."

I looked into her grinning, spiteful face and wanted to scream. But before I did, a voice distracted me.

"Hi, Chris. You all right?"

All at once the anger slipped away and I felt myself turning into a pathetic pile of mush.

"Uh, yeah. . ." I mumbled in response to Sean, as I watched him squeeze past us from the kitchen, can of beer in hand, and head into the diningroom. Once again the Law of Fancying People had struck, where it's impossible to talk in anything like a normal way to the object of your desire.

Dragging my gaze away from his receding back, I turned to face Faith.

"Ahhh. . ." she said knowingly, her expression letting me know that she'd immediately sussed my feelings. She turned to Emma, saying, "C'mon, let's mingle," before leading the way towards the dining-room.

God knows how long I stayed in there, but it felt like sanctuary.

I sat on the loo for ages, my head resting against the cool marble tiles of the wall, trying to calm down. After that, I stood at the sink a while, letting the torrent of cold water run over my wrists and feeling the soothing watery rush slow my racing heartbeat. It wasn't till I heard hammering on the door and Laurie's voice that I finally dragged my wet hands over my face and through my hair and went to open the door.

"Chris! I was worried! Are you OK?" Behind her stood a queue of curious – and presumably desperate – people.

"Sorry," I said, shamefaced, to Laurie and anyone whose bladder I'd inconvenienced.

Once we were in the kitchen, I tried to explain what I thought Faith was up to, but it didn't sound so convincing when I put it into words.

"I don't think Faith's going to try to snog some guy in the year below her just to get at you. She wouldn't see that as a very cool move, would she?

Don't forget that appearances matter to someone like her. Nah, she'll be after some of Katrina's brother's college mates. Trust me, Chris."

"I know, I know," I answered, starting to feel like I'd overreacted a little. "But everything's been spoiled now and I just want to go home. You don't have to come."

"Course I do," she said, giving me a hug. "Let's go get our jackets."

I pulled on my denim jacket in the darkened upstairs hall, while Laurie gave it "one for the road" as she said in the bathroom before we left for the long walk back home.

A breathless gasp made me jump. It's funny how the dark can do that — make you jump at sounds you wouldn't pay any attention to in the daytime. I pussyfooted my way along the corridor towards the source of the sound.

There it was again. How funny! Someone was obviously breaking Brown Owl's strictest rule and getting hot and bothered in one of the untouchable upstairs rooms. I couldn't resist peeking. But even before I'd pushed the door open enough to spy in, I knew who I'd find. He had her pressed against the window-sill, kissing her neck, their outlines illuminated by the light from the conservatory below.

"Faith. Oh, Faith!" Sean practically groaned.

Point Romance

Are you burning with passion, and aching with desire? Then these are the books for you! Point Romance brings you passion, romance, heartache ... and *love*.